a modern Pride and Prejudice story

MCKINLEY JAMES

"In playing ball, and in life, a person occasionally gets the opportunity to do something great. When that time comes, only two things matter: being prepared to seize the moment and having the courage to take your best swing."

– HANK AARON

"To succeed in baseball, as in life, you must make adjustments."

– KEN GRIFFEY JR.

"Love is the most important thing in the world, but baseball is pretty good, too."

– YOGI BERRA

PROLOGUE

Three Years Ago

MAN, he was good.

It was impossible not to notice him, and not just because shortstop was a very visible position. He was fast on his feet, had a good, strong throw and a decent bat, and he clearly loved to play.

She knew who he was—he was a good friend of her cousin's —but as she'd never met him, she preferred to think of him by his position.

She could only vaguely make out his face from her spot in the stands, but she imagined he was handsome. She never got close enough to find out. She only came to the games to watch her cousin; she wasn't interested in meeting any of his teammates.

Or so she told herself.

It had nothing to do with the possibly handsome guy at shortstop, and everything to do with familial support and her own love of the game.

Even as she reminded herself of this, the batter for the opposing team cracked a liner right up the middle, in short's direction. Her heart leapt into her throat, anticipation and pride mixing as Shortstop pivoted, feet a blur as his arm darted out, snagging the ball in his glove even as he reached into it. In a flash, the ball was in his hand, and he whipped it to first in time to throw out the runner who'd made it halfway to second before halting and backtracking.

Double play! And that made three outs.

"Yeah!"

The cheer ripped out of her, pure adrenaline, and she found herself on her feet along with some other members of the crowd, her hands clasping together of their own volition.

Then in a rush, the adrenaline left her when both her cousin and Shortstop turned their heads in her direction as they made their way back to the dugout.

Embarrassed, she plopped her butt back on the bleachers and hoped she blended in enough that he hadn't noticed her.

⚾⚾⚾

HE NOTICED HER. He always noticed her.

She'd come to a lot of their games over the past year, sitting up high in the corner of the stands where she would have a good view of the field, but where she could blend in to the background.

He knew who she was, of course. Her cousin Ryder, their pitcher, talked about her all the time, and had pointed her out. He knew she was a good catcher, and played softball at a private university.

He also surmised, from observation, that she did her best not to draw attention to herself. This wasn't terribly surprising, as Ry's own testimony was she was rather reserved and quiet.

But he noticed her anyway.

And he couldn't shake the mild annoyance that she always left at the very end of the game, after the last out, but before

2

they'd packed up their gear—which meant Ryder couldn't call her down and introduce her to the team.

It was actually pretty sneaky, and he both admired and resented it.

He couldn't put his finger on why he wanted to meet her so badly. Maybe it was simply because Ryder talked about her so much. And though he could imagine her features—he knew she was gorgeous because he'd seen Ryder's pictures—it would be nice to put an in-person face to the woman he'd heard so much about, who was even now only a dark-haired figure in the stands.

And who appeared to be looking in his direction. Maybe it was ridiculous, but his skin pricked a little under her scrutiny, as it always did whenever he noticed her looking his way. He knew she didn't necessarily disapprove; she'd just been applauding the play he made, after all. And maybe she wasn't staring at him at all, but somehow he just knew she was—and it both amused and irked him she stared at him, but made no effort to interact with him.

To tease her, he looked right at her, kept his eyes on her as he tipped his ball cap in salutation. Even from a distance he could see her straighten. He smirked, wishing he could see her expression.

Then he took a few long gulps from his water bottle, turning to sit on the bench as the batting commenced. When he glanced back a few minutes later, she was gone.

It wasn't the last time he'd see her; she came back for other games, and was there for the last game of their college career, cheering and smiling as they brought home a championship. He hadn't acknowledged her presence after that one time, but this time he did.

She was still gone by the time they'd packed up, but his mood was secure in their win, and the memory that this time, when he'd tipped his hat in her direction, she'd nodded back.

ONE

FOR SEVERAL LONG YEARS, the sprawling three-story Victorian mansion, in all its intricately carved, pastel-painted splendor, had sat vacant, with nothing but humble spiders, dust mites, and perhaps the occasional squatter as guests.

But now, Levi Bennet thought as he and his brother climbed its dirt and grime-blanketed porch steps, they'd get to bring the Netherfield Inn back to life.

Jackson rang the bell, and Levi took a moment to glance around the empty wrap-around porch. Already he could tell it desperately needed some sanding, and either some painting or a nice stain, but otherwise it appeared to be in good shape. And he could envision what it would be like for guests to sit outside with a cup of coffee in the morning.

He imagined that was just the sort of thing the new owner had in mind. She'd sounded very enthusiastic about her plans for the neglected B&B, and she'd clicked with Bennet Family Contractors right off the bat. In truth, they'd been itching for the opportunity to revamp the old inn, had even been on the verge of buying it when they'd gotten the news it sold.

Thankfully, Bree Carpenter had hired them for the renovation, and by some miracle, her vision aligned with their own plans. Their father had met with her at their office, and they'd talked to her on the phone a few times, but now they'd be meeting her in person, and walk through the space with her.

When the wide, wooden door opened, a tall, willowy woman with reddish-blonde hair scooped back into a messy bun greeted them with a beaming smile. She was dressed casually in shorts and a t-shirt, and her pale green eyes widened a little when she spotted Jackson, whose stylishly cut dark blonde hair, tall, muscular build, and hazel eyes made him a striking figure.

"Hello! I'm Bree." Her voice was bright and musical, and she held out her hand with genuine pleasure. They each shook it in turn as she continued, "You must be Jackson and Levi Bennet?"

Jackson nodded, a little in awe of the woman in front of them. "I'm Jackson, this is my brother, Levi."

"Family business, I'm all for that," Bree said as she gestured them inside. "You ready to get started?"

"Are we ever," Levi told her.

They spent the next half hour going room by room, discussing ideas and jotting down notes. As an interior designer, Bree knew exactly what she wanted, and had already drawn up some preliminary plans, pulling them up on her tablet as they went through the space. They started upstairs, looking at the guest rooms, and made their way down. Levi was particularly charmed at the idea of making over a nook in the upstairs hall as a library space.

"I can't take credit for that," Bree chuckled. "My friend Ro was adamant I turn that space into a library."

Overall, Levi had to admit he was impressed with her initiative and ideas, and so was Jackson if the admiration in his expression was anything to go by.

As they were moving into the dining room, Bree got a text that made her face light up.

"Ro is here," she explained, and handed Jackson the tablet.

"Why don't you look through this while I go talk to her? I'll be right back."

He and Jackson looked through Bree's plans for the dining room, but as the plans were solid, and the room was in good shape, there wasn't much to discuss. Jackson pulled out his measuring tape and began taking some measurements while they waited, but Levi decided to go find Bree. He couldn't deny he was also curious about her friend, the mysterious Ro-who-insisted-upon-libraries, a sentiment he could only approve of.

As he wandered back into the foyer, he heard voices coming from the kitchen, pivoted to head in that direction.

"Hiring local is good for the town's economy, and bolsters favor with the community," Bree was saying, and he stopped short of opening the swinging door.

"No argument there," came another voice, this one lower and almost gravelly in a way that settled over Levi's skin like a whisper. He suppressed a shiver as he nudged the door open a crack, just enough to peer through. Thankfully, neither woman was facing the door; he could just see Bree's face turned slightly toward him, while all he could see of her friend was the back of her long, dark hair, loosely curled, brown corduroy blazer with pale blue trouser shorts, and fancy gladiator-style sandals.

"But we already know the company my family uses does stellar work," the woman he assumed was Ro continued, "Whereas we don't know the quality of work this business provides. We don't know anything about these guys—"

"I've been talking with them for weeks, Ro." Bree sounded a little exasperated. "Trust me, I've done my research, and they're the best. And after walking around with them I can tell they really know their stuff—and they really care about this place."

"I'm sure they do—"

"One of them really liked your library idea." Bree said this like it was the ace up her sleeve and would magically change her friend's mind.

But Levi could practically hear Ro roll her eyes. "He might've just said that to get on your good side."

Indignation spread through his veins, like cracks of lava through the earth's surface. Who did this city socialite think she was? She'd never even spoken to him or his family, so how would she know what they were like, or how good their work was?

Before he could consider the pros and cons of storming in there and giving her a piece of his mind, she turned slightly, and that indignation caught in his throat with a surge of shock, and what he later recognized as disappointment.

He knew that figure, even though the last time he'd seen her was at his and Ryder's collegiate championship game a little more than a couple years ago. Ryder still talked about her often, but Levi hadn't seen hide nor hair of her since then.

He should have known. Ryder called her Ro all the time, but his brain hadn't made the connection until now. He had no idea why she was here, or why Ryder hadn't mentioned it, but Farrow Darcy was in Morton Grove.

Farrow Darcy, the woman he'd been unable to forget for the past few years, despite never having met her in person.

And apparently she didn't approve of her friend's choice of contractor.

Well, she'd just have to deal, he thought as he quietly moved away from the door and back to the dining room.

"You find Bree?" Jackson asked, his face suspiciously hopeful as he glanced up from Bree's tablet.

"She's in the kitchen with her friend."

He didn't explain any further, but there was no need. Jackson simply nodded, and a minute or so later, Bree reentered the room—alone.

Levi was tempted to ask her where her friend was, but didn't want to put her on the spot. Besides, he needed some time to process.

Thankfully, tomorrow was Saturday, and he could work off

some of this confusion and frustration at baseball practice. And when he saw Ryder, maybe he could grill his friend about his cousin—if he could figure out how to do so without making it seem like he was interested.

⚾⚾⚾

AS THE CLEATS he'd dusted off that morning touched down on the field's freshly mowed outfield, Levi took a moment to breathe in the sweet, twangy scent of the grass; that, mixed with notes of the subtle, earthy clay of the infield dirt, invoked the kind of warm nostalgic feeling he was pretty sure you could only feel while on a baseball field.

He felt it on and off every spring and summer. The first time he stepped onto the field for the season, during random moments playing catch, while eating an after-game hot dog—sometimes even just catching sight of a baseball field during the off-season.

There was just something about baseball that dug in and stuck with you.

They got it, Levi thought as his teammates started filtering onto the field. They were all here to play, just because they loved it.

It'd been a couple years since he and Ryder had been released into the quote-unquote 'real world,' leaving exams, papers, and collegiate ball behind to face adulting. Though some Frontier League teams were nearby, they'd both decided not to pursue professional baseball. But that didn't mean they had to give up the game altogether.

They were fortunate enough to live in an area where competitive adult leagues were established and thriving. They'd had no problem joining the Chicagoland Adult Baseball Association's Tier A league for twenty-somethings, and getting placed on a team with likeminded individuals.

Their team, the Longhorns, had been pretty good the past

couple years, but this year they could be the best—he had a feeling.

He hooked his gear bag to the dugout fence, pulled out his maroon ball cap and tugged it down over his waving mop of light brown hair as charcoal gray eyes scanned the field.

His daydreaming was interrupted when his phone buzzed in his pocket; he frowned, pushing back the automatic worry when he saw his brother was calling. Jackson hated phone calls, and he should be at practice by now. Come to think of it, their coach, Andrew, and another teammate seemed to be running late as well.

"Hey," Jackson said when Levi answered. "Everything's fine, but Frank fell off a ladder, and Andrew and I are at the hospital with his wife. We'll head over in a few minutes. Don't tell the others yet, except Ryder—we'll explain when we get there."

"Alright. We'll get practice started," Levi assured him, though his stomach sank with anxiety for their catcher, Frank. Jackson hadn't said whether or not he was injured, but the fact he was in the hospital didn't sound good.

Trying not to think too much about it, he hung up with Jackson and relayed the information to Ryder, who took charge of their practice.

After a warm up run that consisted of a couple laps around the field, they headed back for their gloves to warm up their arms.

"Ready?" Ryder asked Levi, tossing him a ball.

Levi caught it with his ungloved hand, ran his fingers over the familiar red seams, the dirt-covered leather. "You bet."

"By the way, my cousin Ro is in town." Ryder slapped his friend on the back on their way out of the dugout. "You could finally meet her."

Levi kept his voice neutral, turning his head a little so his friend wouldn't see his smile was strained. "Cool."

They jogged out to the outfield with the rest of their teammates, and when they were several yards apart, Levi let the ball fly, watched it sail true, and heard the resounding *smack* in Ryder's glove. They tossed the ball, the warm-up routine familiar and ingrained. The more he felt his arm loosen, the more he slid into the game, and the less he thought about Frank's possible injury and Farrow Darcy.

"It's going to be a good season," his friend declared. The ball smacked into Ryder's glove at eye level. "I can feel it."

Levi felt the quick answering sting of the ball when Ryder whipped it back, but it was a good, satisfying sting—the kind that came from fielding a good, hard throw. The kind that echoed Ryder's sentiment.

They'd been on the same team for years now; that part was no different. But, Levi thought with a glance at the dugout, this year Ryder's cousin Andrew—who'd been injured during a game his senior year of college and no longer played full out—was the coach of their team, and Jackson was team captain. Some of the guys might rag on them about it—playing favorites, that sort of thing, as he'd experienced with coaches in the past—but the guys knew Jackson and Andrew were fair, and that Ryder was one of the best pitchers in the league, so he wasn't worried about it.

In fact, he was looking forward to it.

"You say that every year," he called to Ryder as he returned the throw.

Ryder called back as he snagged the ball. "Yeah, well, am I ever wrong?"

Levi was trying to think of a smart-ass reply when one of the other players cried out.

"Hey, check out the hottie!"

Ryder dropped his arm before he could throw, and he and Levi turned. Billy Collins, the player who'd called out, gestured toward the outfield fence, where a figure leaned against the chain-link, arms resting on the yellow ridged plastic rim.

Levi's stomach dropped, both in anticipation and trepidation.

And, okay, that flare of indignation. He wasn't sure how to feel about her sudden appearance; not only had she come to a practice, she'd actually approached the field and seemed inclined to say hello.

That was a first.

Though it had to be in the mid-seventies, she wore slim jeans that flared at the bottom, a gaping hole in one of the knees, a plain blue-jean ball cap, and a dark gray V-neck tee that somehow managed to look loose without looking baggy. He was just close enough to see the jeans were a little too long on her, so only the front half of her orange Chucks were visible.

It was a complete contrast to her outfit from the day before, giving Levi a kind of mental whiplash.

Ryder's grin broke out at the spurt of recognition, and she lifted a hand in an enthusiastic wave. He waved back, and Billy wiggled his eyebrows. "You know her?"

"Yeah, that's my cousin, Farrow." Ryder noticed the others had stopped warming up, too, glancing between him and Farrow, who, with the ease of experience, had hoisted herself onto the fence instead of going through the gate when Ryder gestured for her to come over. She dropped down as Levi jogged over to Ryder's side.

"Did you invite her?" Levi asked.

"Yeah."

Levi nodded, almost absentmindedly; to Ryder, the look on his friend's face seemed simultaneously annoyed and eager.

How curious.

The rest of the players had gathered around them, Billy letting out a low whistle as Farrow walked toward them, the slight breeze playing with her long chestnut hair—so similar to Ry's—under her cap.

"Your cousin's hot."

"Hey," Ryder growled, and even Levi's stomach tightened,

just a little, at the predatory look on Billy's face. "Don't make me throw this ball at you."

Billy shrugged. "I'm just saying. I'd tap that."

Ryder narrowed his eyes. "Dude. Seriously."

"Hey!" Farrow called out as she stepped up to the huddle. Out of habit, Ryder tossed her the ball in his hand; she caught it with one hand, immediately began fiddling with it. "Thought I'd come by and see you and Andrew in action. Where is he, anyway?"

"He and our captain had an errand and are running late," Ryder explained without batting an eye. "We're just finishing warming up. Guys, this is my cousin Farrow; Ro, this is the team."

"I can see that," she smirked a little, though Levi thought she was deliberately avoiding looking directly at him, which only irritated him more. "Anyway, don't let me interrupt practice; I'll just go hang out in the dugout."

"Why don't you join us?"

Levi caught the flash of surprise on her face, one that mirrored Ryder's as he turned to Levi. Levi just grinned; though he was surprised at himself as well, he was curious why she was here, and why she was suddenly more sociable—or at least, slightly more sociable. And he could admit he was getting a kick out of putting Miss High and Mighty on the spot.

"Frank isn't here yet, so you'll need someone to catch for you," he said to Ryder, noting his friend's raised brow at the mention of Frank. Perhaps he was getting his hopes up about Frank's condition. "And I, for one, would like to see the Dynamic Duo in action."

Before Ryder could speak, Billy snorted. "Her? Catch for *Ryder*? Yeah, right."

A particular gleam came into Ro's crystalline blue eyes—one Levi had often seen in his friend Cristina's when she had a point to prove. Something told him Farrow wasn't the type to

13

back down from a challenge; he wasn't sure what that meant for the one he'd inadvertently issued.

Uh-oh, was all he could think.

"Let me guess." To anyone paying attention, Ro's smile was deceptively calm. "You don't think girls can play baseball."

"Not real baseball," Billy said, and Ro arched an eyebrow. "And there's a reason Ryder here is known as 'Torch.' Even Frank has a hard time keeping up with him sometimes."

"There's also a reason our cousin Andrew calls us the Dynamic Duo." Ro carefully kept her smirk in place as she looked at Ryder, who suspected he was the only one who could see the hint of annoyance behind her eyes. He thought of all the times he'd heard Billy talk about how the sports skills of women were inferior, of how each time he'd thought of mentioning Ro, who was the best catcher he knew, but never did.

He'd always sort of thought Billy was a jerk with a pubescent mind, but he'd ignored it because he played the game well. Maybe that had been a mistake. Now, as the annoyance he sensed in Ro became a question, he thought of Levi's request. It might be fun to prove Billy wrong.

He grinned, nodded at her. "Fortunately, the Dynamic Duo's have been in action for several years. Got your glove with you, Vac?"

She rolled her eyes at the nickname, but grinned back. "Always. Where's the gear?"

"In the dugout."

"Got it. Be right back." She turned and headed back toward the fence, and Ryder gestured toward the infield.

"'Kay, guys," he said as he headed in. "Guess it's time for some infield practice."

ⓍⓍⓍⓍⓍ

FARROW FELT her temper lodge in her gut as she walked to her car, opened it. Why did guys always think she was inferior just because she was female? As far as she was concerned that shouldn't mean squat.

And yet, she'd had to work three times as hard as any man just to get people to take her seriously, even in her family's own company. Unfortunately, a lot of people—her own uncle included—often dismissed her as nothing but a silly little heiress.

Boy did she love proving them wrong.

She'd go along with the plans for The Pemberley hotel chain, but she also had plans of her own, starting with helping Bree with the Netherfield Inn. She didn't care what Andrew's snooty father had to say about that. It was her own endeavor, hers and Bree's, and had nothing to do with Pemberley.

Baseball—and softball—had often been her escape from worldly pressures, familial expectations, and the general anxiety of life. So it was a slap to the face to have some dude belittle what was sacred to her.

She felt the knot loosen to anticipation as she pulled her catcher's mitt from her gear bag. It had been a little while since she'd played catch with Ryder, but they never missed a beat. And crouching behind home plate was, for her—well, home.

She glanced down at her shoes, decided it would probably be better if she wore her cleats. With that, she slung her gear bag over her shoulder, locked her car.

When she reached the dugout, Ryder was there with one of the other players, pulling out the catcher's gear; the rest of the team was warming up in the infield, though she noticed short-stop was empty.

Naturally, it would be him. Shortstop. She'd thought she'd recognized his gait, his ease with Ryder, but it'd been so long since she'd seen him she couldn't be sure. Now there was no doubt in her mind, and she did her best not to let the reality of him distract her.

She could feel some of the team watching her, though it seemed mostly from curiosity, except for the smug arrogance coming from second.

"You're really going to have to adjust these straps, Short Stack," Ryder said to her as she sat on the metal bench, tugged at her shoe laces.

She stuck her tongue out at him. "Used to it."

Shortstop, his sun-lightened brown hair curling a bit around his ears and under his ball cap, set the catcher's mask next to her. She'd been right all those years ago—he was certainly very handsome. She hoped she didn't look like a lovestruck puppy.

"I'm Levi, by the way," he said, holding out a hand.

She shook it firmly, as had been ingrained into her, even as her heart slapped against her chest cavity, then began putting her cleats on. "Levi Bennet?"

He gave her a charming grin she thought only movie stars could pull off, wiggled his brows over gray eyes that reflected all the surrounding colors like mirrors. "Heard of me, have you?"

Though she mentally kicked herself when she realized there was another reason she'd heard the name Bennet, it was impossible not to smile back. "If you're the Levi Bennet Ryder's been telling me about for the past several years. I was starting to get jealous."

"Back at you."

There was something else behind the words, under the tone and the charm. Something testing and inquisitive, but she didn't have time to examine it at the moment.

"Hey, stop flirting with my cousin." Ryder's voice was a little exasperated, reminding her of a cloud of exhaust puffing out of a tired engine as he dropped the gear in front her. As she finished tying her laces, she kept her gaze from his all-too-observant eye. "And you, stop flirting with my friend."

"No guarantees, bro." Levi slapped Ryder's shoulder, sent Ro a wink. Before she had time examine what that meant, or what his wry smile did to her, his face sobered a little. "In all seriousness, though, I expect you to wipe that smirk off Billy's prickish face."

She spared a glance at the second baseman, who caught her looking. "You done primping yet, sweetheart? We haven't got all day," he called out. She heard some of the other players chuckle and decided she wouldn't dignify the question with a response.

"That guy?" she asked Levi.

"Yeah."

"My pleasure."

She started with the shin guards first, clipping them into place and tugging the straps tight. She was pulling the chest protector over her head when a familiar blue Jeep and an unfamiliar black pickup pulled into the parking lot.

A lanky man she recognized as her other cousin got out of the Jeep, slid a maroon cap onto his head over his shortly cropped ginger hair. The other guy, who she assumed was Jackson Bennet—Levi's older brother, if she remembered Ryder and Bree's info correctly—stepped out of the truck, hailed them as they headed toward the dugout. The rest of the team started heading in, too, when Andrew called out, "Bring it in, guys."

"Hey, Andrew," Farrow greeted him as he approached.

"Farrow." Though he was clearly surprised, Andrew smiled at her. "What's going on?"

"Ro came to visit," Ryder told him. "And since Frank isn't here yet, I thought she could catch for us." He deliberately left out the part about Billy's taunting Ro. Though you wouldn't know it from his build, Andrew could be a bear if you angered him.

Jackson nodded, but his mind seemed to be somewhere else. The team had filed into the dugout by that time; now they stood, waiting for him to say something as he took off his cap to run his fingers through thick, dirty blonde hair before setting it back on his head.

17

"Right," he finally said, mostly to himself. He rubbed the back of his neck, looked up at the team. "About Frank. We were just at the hospital. He's in the emergency room getting a cast on a broken arm."

"What happened?" One of the players asked.

"Apparently he was helping his father clean his gutters this morning, and fell off the ladder," Andrew informed them. "Obviously, he won't be able to play this season. We have to think about what that means for the team."

Ryder looked at Ro, laid a hand on her shoulder. "You picked a hell of a day for a visit. Think you can do some filling in today?"

"C'mon, Ryder." Billy straightened from where he leaned against the dugout wall. "You can't be serious."

"I'm always serious about baseball, Billy." Knowing Ro, he kept a firm hand on the shoulder of the chest protector to keep her in place. "Trust me, Farrow here will be a big help today."

Nodding in agreement, Andrew chipped in. "Why don't we do some fielding drills?"

He and Jackson assigned players to the other eight positions, with the remaining players acting as runners. When they headed into the field, Ro took off her cap and pulled the hair tie from around her wrist, began to twist her hair back in a pony-tail; and when Jackson went to grab a bat and a bucket of balls, Billy gave her a smug wink.

"Try not to break a nail."

Real original, she thought, giving him a silky sweet smile expertly laced with acid. She pumped that same acid into the tone of her voice as she held up her hands, nails out, so he could clearly see they were cut short.

"I don't have any nails to break." She folded her fingers inward so that only her middle finger remained. "Sweetheart."

Billy scowled for a moment, but chuckled as he walked out to second. Levi, clearly amused at the interaction, gave her an encouraging smile and nod before taking his place at short. As the runners grabbed batting helmets, Ro picked up the catcher's mask.

"Hm," Ryder said, frowning. "That might be a little big for you."

Nodding, Ro simply hiked up her ponytail a nudge, picked up her cap, placed it on backward. "I'll make it work."

He held out his fist; she bumped it with her own before placing the helmet on her head, picking up her glove. She waddled out to take her place behind the plate—the fit of the gear was a little restricting, but since she was petite, that was pretty much always the case.

But she'd never felt awkward in the thick, padded gear. It had always felt right. Though nothing felt more right than a glove on her hand, she thought as she slipped hers on.

Andrew already stood at the plate, a bat on his shoulder. He reached into the bucket behind him as she faced the diamond, sat back on her haunches.

"Ready?" he asked her.

"Play ball," she said with a smirk, and slid the mask down over her face.

They spent a half hour or so fielding the flies and grounders Andrew hit their way, working on the plays he called out, including some at home. Between plays, he instructed the runners with hand signals. He switched up the runners, switched up positions a couple times, including putting one of the other players on short, Levi on second, and Billy at the pitcher's mound. Billy barely acknowledged her, but she imagined he wished he could purposefully throw her a stray pitch.

Then they switched up positions again, and Ryder moved back to the mound.

"I'm going to warm up a little," he told her, grinning. "Nothing fancy today, just sticking to fastballs."

From her crouch, she gave him a thumbs up, readying her glove.

From shortstop, Levi watched them, Ryder's throws getting

harder with each pitch. He heard each one make that familiar satisfying smack into Ro's glove.

It was sort of like magic, he thought. He knew Ryder's pitches could go wild when he got too nervous, but with Ro behind the plate he seemed calmer.

And Ro? Jesus, she could move.

Sometimes without hardly seeming to move at all. He winced a little as the next pitch went a little low, bounced up from the dirt in front of the plate.

But Ro went to her knees, scooped it right up—like a vacuum cleaner. *The Vac.* He grinned to himself, admiration reluctantly worming its way inside him.

They were a unit, the two cousins who loved baseball. You only had to watch to know it, to realize they'd probably been the Dynamic Duo longer than most people knew. As good a catcher as Frank was, he'd never have the bond with Ryder that Ro did—no one would. And though he was sorry he'd be stuck spending time with someone who thought so little of his family, and sorrier about Frank's injury, he couldn't help the thought that popped into his head.

Maybe there was a little bit of fate in the works.

Some might find the thought corny, or ridiculous, he knew— Billy certainly would—but it seemed to him that sometimes baseball was just as much about fate as it was about practice, faith, skill, and luck.

After a few more pitches, Ryder nodded. "I'm good."

Andrew had the current runners get up to bat, getting them to make plays for a few rounds before suggesting they practice plays for a runner stealing a base. He looked at Levi. "Be ready at two."

Levi grinned and nodded, but Billy, now the runner at first, sputtered out a laugh. "There's no way the chick can throw that far."

Ro couldn't quite resist the urge to grind her teeth, though she heard the first baseman—Henry, she remembered Andrew calling him—hiss out, *"Shut up, man."* She heard the sternness in Andrew's voice, a bit like he was scolding a misbehaving child, when he said, "That's enough, Billy," and called the play: Billy would attempt to steal second sliding in, Ro would make the throw to Levi.

When her eyes met Ryder's, he gave her a nod. To her the nod said, *Let's kick his ass—metaphorically speaking, of course.* In response, she pounded a fist in her glove, held it at the ready. Let out a slow breath.

Ryder wound up, hitched his leg. The moment the ball left his hand, Billy shot off the bag. The ball hit her glove in less than a second, and she was already pivoting, her arm reaching into her glove for the ball even as she brought it back for the throw.

Instead of taking a step—which used up precious half-seconds—she used the momentum of her torso to put force behind the throw, hurling the ball toward second just as Levi reached it. He caught it, turning, and was about to crouch to tag the runner on a sweep, when he noticed that Billy hadn't even bothered to slide. So he simply stood over the base, glove out in front of him.

And Billy barreled into him.

They both hit the ground on a groan. Heart pounding, Ro immediately ripped off her mask and mitt as Andrew and the rest of the team hurried over to where the two men were sitting up. Billy removed his helmet as Levi held up his glove, the ball still snug in its web.

"You're out, asshole."

"Levi." Jackson gave him a shake of the head as Ryder helped him up. "There's no need to call each other names."

But Ryder's fury was barely restrained, the taut chains around it about to snap as he looked at Billy, who had already gotten to his feet.

"Would you like to tell me why you ignored the instructions

to slide? You could have seriously injured yourself, and Levi, and we're already down a team member."

"He didn't think he'd need to," Ro said, folding her arms over the chest protector. "I can't throw that far, remember? Hell, I'm surprised he didn't just walk to second."

Billy, for once, was silent. She couldn't read his face either. He seemed pissed, of course, and maybe…embarrassed? Sheepish? Maybe that was just wishful thinking.

Andrew sighed. "Okay, guys. I think that's enough for today."

But he held Billy back with a friendly but firm hand to his shoulder, speaking to him in low tones while the others headed in.

Ro went to retrieve her glove and mask from where she'd dropped them before carrying them to the dugout; she began removing the catcher's gear as the others picked up and stowed the rest of the gear. The dugout was quiet but for the muffled thumps of packing up and the zipping of gear bags, until Levi cleared his throat.

"I have a suggestion."

"What?" Jackson asked.

"I think Farrow should join the team."

He watched as Ro paused in the act of shoving the chest protector into the large canvas bag that held the catcher's gear and batting helmets, looked up at him in astonishment. The dugout had gone silent; even Billy looked on, too dumbfounded to think of anything to say. Ryder exchanged a considering look with Jackson before turning the same one on Andrew.

"Me?" Ro straightened. "Are women even allowed in this league?"

"Technically, it's a men's league," Brandon, their right fielder, shared. "But it's not labeled as one, and as far as we know, there are no rules against female players."

Fred, their left fielder, held up the bat he was stowing away. "What about batting? We haven't even seen her hit, or run."

"Man," Henry shook his head. "If she can hit half as good as she catches, we'll be fine."

"Trust me," said Ryder. "She can."

"Excuse me?" Ro raised her hand. "Still here. I haven't even said if I'd like to join the team."

"Would you?" asked Ryder, raising his brows.

"I'd have to think about it."

She'd tried to sound stern, Levi noted, but she couldn't meet her cousin's eyes. Ryder himself didn't seem surprised by this, simply nodding his head as though he'd expected her answer. Levi knew it was practical for her to think about it before giving an answer—she did have other obligations, after all—but the disappointment he felt at the idea of her not playing with them was palpable.

What was wrong with him?

He snapped out of this train of thought when Ryder spoke again.

"Our next practice isn't for a couple days," Ryder was saying. "Why don't you get back to us by then?"

Ro bit her lip, but nodded. "Sounds good."

"Okay, everyone. Practice Monday, same time." Andrew clapped his hands, breaking up the huddle. As everyone went back to packing up, he glanced back at Ro, amused. "I think you can put those shin guards away now."

She looked down at her gear-clad legs, smirking when she raised her head. "You got it. *Coach*."

TWO

KNOWING full well Jackson would want to go check up on Frank, Levi asked Ryder if he'd want to come over as they picked their way over the gravel lot to their cars.

"I'm just going to hang the rest of the day," he said as they threw their gear in their trunks.

Ryder assented, then, with a gimlet eye on Levi, smirked at Ro, who'd stowed her own gear and was opening her car door. "Wanna join?"

She smiled, amused, but paused. "Not if you're just going to sit around and play video games."

"Hey, video games are a great way to relax after a long day, and simultaneously let off some steam," Ryder told her.

"I don't doubt it. But I suck at video games."

He couldn't argue with that. "This is true."

"You could watch."

Ro's brow quirked as she tilted her head at Levi. "And do what, cheer you on? Giggle and squeal when you kick Ry's ass?"

"Hey!" Ryder objected.

"You don't strike me as the giggle-and-squeal type."

"Oh? And what type am I?"

Ryder rolled his eyes. "If you guys are gonna flirt, can you at least do it when I'm not present?"

He noted the faint blush creeping into Ro's cheeks even as she frowned.

"Told you man, no guarantees." Levi's tone was light, but suggested he knew exactly what he was doing, causing Ryder to lift a brow. "Besides, we're not flirting; I'm just teasing."

Ryder turned the brow on Farrow.

"I don't flirt," she deadpanned, her voice and expression indicating there was no hell in which she would stoop to that level of social interaction.

They weren't prevaricating, Ryder supposed; either they were both in denial, or they were both totally oblivious. Yes, Levi often teased, and Ro would rather eat pig's feet than flirt. But he was close enough to both of them to notice how they each paid more attention when he talked about them to each other over the years, to know how aware they'd been of each other when she'd come to watch their games in college.

And to note the glances they'd been sending each other since Ro had appeared at the fence.

Yet they both hedged around what appeared to him to be genuine interest instead of acting on that interest.

Curiouser and curiouser.

But he let it go—for now. The harder he teased Ro, the more she'd shut down, and Levi would never admit to something he didn't want to, or wasn't ready for. Levi wasn't as good at hiding his feelings as he thought, though; Ryder watched him watch Farrow as she bid them goodbye, climbed into her car, and drove away.

His friend was interested Ro, whether he knew it or not.

⁑⁂⁑

"OH, FUCK OFF!"

Grinning wickedly, Levi watched his character, Yoshi, travel via golden pipe to the space with the star, and Levi bought it. Ryder continued to curse when he saw how far away the next star moved from his character, Luigi.

"You're killing me. You're killing me, Smalls."

"Are you really that surprised?" asked Tina.

Cristina Lucado, Levi's best friend since first grade, merely shook her head at Ryder, pure amusement lighting her face.

The three of them were ensconced on the black velvet couch —which had seen better days, but which was remarkably comfortable, and thus, made them reluctant to replace it—in Levi and Jackson's apartment, playing a rather rousing game of Mario Party. The game had been Cristina's suggestion, and Ryder had agreed, even though they both knew the chances Levi would kick their butts was relatively high.

"No," Ryder grumbled as Tina took her turn, and they watched as Princess Daisy punched a five from her dice. "But it doesn't change the fact that our boy here is evil."

"Aw, *pobrecito*," Tina pouted her lower lip, her tone still amused and containing zero sympathy.

Ryder shot her an indignant glare and continued, "What kind of sick bastard steals a star from under someone's nose just as they're about to reach it?"

"Pretty much anyone who's ever played Mario Party," Tina reminded him. "Including you."

"Yeah, yeah." Ryder only grumbled more when Levi gave him a smug look. "One of these days, someone is going to own you, Levi."

"Maybe." Levi only shrugged. "But not today."

After Ryder's turn gave them a mini game, he decided a change of subject was in order, especially if it was one he knew would rattle Levi.

Keeping his voice casual, he said, "So what do you think now that you've finally met Farrow in person?"

Levi flinched a little, and Tina whipped her head around to stare at them, her soft brown eyes widening a little from under her jet black bangs before zoning in on Levi. "You met Farrow? When? Why didn't you say anything?"

Levi heard the unspoken *why didn't you tell me* and winced a little. Cristina had heard Ryder talk about his cousin several times, and so was just as curious as Levi had been; but as his closest friend, she was also the one with whom Levi had shared his unidentified feelings—such as the odd connection he felt to Ro, despite never having met her. Now that he had met her, his feelings were even more jumbled, and he didn't like it.

Farrow Darcy sparked something in him, but he had yet to determine what, and he wasn't entirely sure he could explain that to Tina, especially in front of Ryder.

Fortunately, Ryder answered for him.

"At practice today. She stopped by and ended up practicing with us," he explained, and Levi mused that it wasn't technically untrue—he hadn't actually met her until practice. Besides, Ryder would only write off Ro's rudeness with some excuse, and he didn't want to make it a big deal, so he decided to take inspiration from Tina and exercise some diplomacy.

As they wrapped up their game, Ryder told Tina about Frank's accident, the events of their practice, and Levi's suggestion Ro take Frank's place.

At this, Tina turned a speculative eye on Levi, and he hunched a little under her discerning gaze. Why he was suddenly uncomfortable he couldn't say, but nothing about Farrow's arrival had been comfortable, so perhaps it was just a side effect.

"Well I hope she decides to join," Tina said. "It sounds like you could use her."

"Boy could we," Ryder agreed.

"But you didn't say what she's doing in town," Tina pointed out.

Ryder set down his controller, excitement lighting his features. "Her friend Bree bought this old B&B, and they're going to fix it up and reopen it."

27

"The Netherfield Inn?" Tina guessed, watching Levi carefully.

"Yeah, how'd you know?"

Levi answered before she could. "That's the inn my family was looking at."

"Oh." Ryder's excitement dimmed. "Damn it, I didn't think…they probably learned about the place from me. Sorry, man."

"It's okay," Levi assured him, not meeting either of his friends' eyes. "Bree hired Bennet Family Contractors to do the renovations, so we've still got a hand in it."

Though he felt Cristina's attention was still on him, she asked Ryder, "If Bree bought the inn, what is Farrow doing here?"

"To help Bree out, mostly. You already know Ro's family owns a chain of boutique hotels, so she's got the expertise to guide Bree in the hospitality industry," Ryder explained. "And Bree's a brilliant interior designer, so I don't doubt she's got great plans for the place."

"She does," Levi confirmed. "Jax and I met her this morning, and we did a walkthrough with her. She's already drawn up her ideas."

Ryder's eyebrows shot up. "You met her, too? What'd you think?"

"She's super nice." Levi relaxed, as he had genuinely like Bree. "And very pretty. She's personable, and I get the impression she makes friends easily; and even just based on our one meeting, I think she clearly knows what she's doing with the reno. A lot of her ideas aligned with what we had in mind for the place. Jax and I were thoroughly impressed. I liked her."

Tina arched a brow. "I take it Jackson liked her, too?"

Levi gave an affirming nod. "He did, and the feeling appears to be mutual. Her eyes lit up like a Christmas tree when she saw him."

Tina chuckled knowingly. Jackson's good looks drew a lot of attention, whether he wanted it or not.

"Well, that's not terribly surprising," Ryder rolled his eyes. "Jackson has that effect on people."

If Levi didn't know better, he would've thought he detected a hint of jealousy in Ry's tone. And perhaps there was a little; he and Levi were often overlooked when standing next to Jackson, but neither of them had ever held it against him. The fact was, they were just used to it, and often amused by Jackson's obliviousness.

"So, anything of note with the renovation?" Tina inquired.

"Actually, yeah." Levi leaned back and grinned. "There's this nook space in the second floor hallway where Bree wants to put a little library."

Ryder grinned back. "A library? That had to be Ro's idea."

"It was," Levi said, a little less enthusiastically; if Ryder or Tina noticed, neither said anything, though he could feel Cristina assessing him again and endeavored to keep a straight face.

"Any idea when the reno will start?" Ryder asked. "Ro's been pretty tight-lipped, and surprisingly, so has Bree."

Levi shook his head. "I guess I'll find out on Monday."

⟨⟨⟨⟨⟨⟩

"THAT'S AWESOME!"

The two friends in question were having a similar discussion in the kitchen of Bree's colorful, boho apartment. After discussing the plans for the inn for a bit, Farrow had told Bree the story of the events of the day, and Bree had responded to the idea with her usual enthusiasm.

Bree, who was currently whipping up something for dinner that smelled heavenly, turned to look at Ro, who was busy pouring them each a glass of wine.

"Is it?"

Bree rolled her eyes. "You love baseball. And you and Ryder have always lamented not being able to play on the same team. Why not go for it?"

Both things were true. But there was one thing Bree was overlooking. "You know why," Ro frowned as she handed Bree her glass.

"You can't let that hold you back." Bree poured the home-made pesto she'd blended onto some pasta. "You already let him take something you love from you once. Don't give him the satisfaction of missing out on it again."

To distract herself, Farrow took her time getting out plates and silverware for the two of them.

"I know you're right," she finally said. "It just brings back some hard memories."

"So replace it with better ones."

She said it so casually, it took Farrow a moment to realize what the suggestion truly meant. She couldn't erase her memories, but she could build new ones. And if she continued to forgo something she loved because of a painful past experience, she was letting her past dictate her future.

She would be letting *him* win.

Bree knew her friend well enough not to be bothered by her silence, and simply waited for Ro to think it through. Since she'd plated the food while Ro was lost in thought, she happened to be watching her, and caught the moment resolve appeared on Ro's features.

It was enough for now, Bree decided, that Ro was thinking about it instead of brushing it off. It'd been too long since her friend had really done something for herself, always focusing on what she could do for those around her.

It was an admirable trait, and she was more grateful for Ro's help than she could say. But it had also been hard to watch her close herself off, until all but surface levels of emotion were bricked up behind masks of calm and competence.

She'd poke that fire carefully, she thought as she and Ro sat down to eat, and do what she could to bring her friend back out of her shell.

She took a sip of wine as she regarded Ro's averted gaze, and shifted the subject slightly. "So, you met the Bennet brothers?"

"I did."

Bree waited a beat as Farrow took a bite of her pasta, said nothing more.

Okay, looked like she'd have to prod a little harder.

"And?" She prompted. "Thoughts? Impressions?"

This got a smirk. "You just want me to tell you I think they're hot."

"Well, yeah, I could see that for myself," Bree grinned. "But what else? Still have reservations about them working on the inn?"

The smirk disappeared, replaced with a contemplative frown.

"Right. I'd forgotten about that." Farrow sighed. "Jackson seems to have a good head on his shoulders, and Levi..."

He had mischievous eyes, she thought. And she couldn't say why, but it pulled at her.

"He's intelligent," she finally decided on. "If they're both half as good contractors as they are ball players, the inn should be in good hands."

Not what you were going to say, Bree noted, but kept the thought to herself. "Good. Then when I meet with them on Monday, we'll lay out a schedule. Are you still thinking you want to partner with me on this?"

She was about to dig back into her food, and Ro was about to respond, when her buzzer sounded.

"Hold that thought." She rose to go answer, pressed the intercom button. "Hello?"

The voice sounded a little tinny through the speaker. "It's Ry. Is Ro there?"

"She is." Though her heart stuttered a bit—Ryder Williams

just did that to her—years of practice enabled her to keep her voice even. "We're having girl time. Why should I let you in?"

"I brought your favorite wine."

Damn it, that was a good reason. She pressed the button to let him in, then walked back to the kitchen.

"Your cousin decided to visit," she told Ro. "He's looking for you."

Ro doubted that was entirely the case, but she gave her friend an apologetic look. "Sorry. I mentioned to him I was coming here tonight."

"It's fine, there's plenty of pasta. And he had the decency to bring my favorite wine to butter me up."

"Did he?" Farrow didn't bother to hide her smirk.

"No, stop that." Bree pointed a finger at her friend, then turned away at the sound of a knock at the door. "He's not here for me."

You keep telling yourself that, Farrow thought as Bree went to answer it.

When she reentered carrying a bottle of wine, a beaming Ryder trailing behind her, Farrow raised a brow. "To what do I owe the pleasure, oh cousin of mine?"

"Obviously I'm here to convince you to join the team," Ryder said, folding his arms.

"You could do that at any time," Farrow pointed out. "Yet, here you are."

Ryder cleared his throat, deliberately not looking at Bree. "Yes, well. The sooner I get to you, the better."

"Questions first."

Ryder nodded for her to continue.

"The park where you practice, is that where games are held?"

"No, those fields are just for practice. Games are hosted by different local high schools and community colleges. We usually play at the Oakton Community College field."

So, not terribly far from the inn, she noted, then continued,

"And I forgot to ask what the league's qualifications are. Do I have the experience necessary to play?"

"We wouldn't be discussing this if you didn't," Ryder said, a little exasperated. "But yes, to clarify. Tier C is recreational, and Tier B is high school or collegiate experience. Our league is Tier A, which is players with collegiate or pro levels of experience."

Pro? Well that wasn't intimidating at all, Farrow thought. But, she might as well listen to what Ryder had to say.

"Alright, then." Farrow set down her fork, picked up her wine glass. "Hit me."

"Well, for starters, I thought you should know Andrew's double checking with the CABA board about the rules. We don't want there to be any doubt there's no rule against female players in the league. So far it seems like it's not usual, but they'll allow it."

"Good to know."

"Second," Ryder continued, pacing a little now. "I know you haven't really played in a while, and I know you miss it. This is the perfect opportunity."

"A fair point," Farrow acknowledged with a sip of her wine.

"And third." Ryder stopped, met her eyes. "We need you, Ro. We need your skills, and you know damn well there's no better catcher for me than you. It would mean a lot to me."

"I know it would." Sighing, Farrow set her glass down. "Look, I've been considering all those points, and I'll keep considering them. But I'm not going to make a decision tonight. Bree and I have other things to discuss."

Ryder nodded. "And I'm interrupting."

"You are, but it doesn't follow that the interruption is unwelcome." Bree held out a plate of pasta to him, smiled. "Now that you're here you have to help us eat all this pasta. I made enough for an army."

"That's because you like leftovers," Ryder grinned back, his bright blue eyes on her smiling lips and flushed cheeks as he took the plate. "But I never turn down a home cooked meal."

Farrow watched the interaction with a quiet smile. Ryder got the dopiest look sometimes when he looked at Bree, and she could swear there were cartoon sparkles in Bree's eyes. But, she thought with a twinge of sadness, that was all it ever was. She didn't understand it.

Finally remembering they weren't alone, Ryder blinked, turned back to Farrow. "So what were you discussing? The inn?"

He pulled out a chair and sat as Bree retook her seat, quietly shoveled a large forkful of pasta into her mouth.

"Yes," Farrow said, eyes darting back and forth between them before settling on Ryder. "I'm considering entering into a partnership with Bree on the inn."

"You mean, like an investor?"

"Like co-owners," Bree informed him, having found her voice.

"Okay." Ryder inclined his head. "Why, though? Haven't you got enough on your plate with Pemberley?"

Farrow sighed. "That's the thing. I love Pemberley, but it doesn't really feel like mine. Pemberley is a family thing—I want to branch out from that. Do my own thing."

"And that's co-owning a bed and breakfast in a Chicago suburb?" Ryder asked, inhaling some pasta.

"Maybe." Farrow shrugged. "Like with the baseball team, nothing's been decided yet."

But she loved the idea of both. She couldn't wait for Bree's plans for the inn to come to fruition, and she planned to be as much a part of it as possible, even if she decided not to take on ownership.

And she really did miss the game; there was a particular ache in her heart whenever she thought about it. Maybe it was time to take a chance.

Ryder only stayed about a half hour, enough for them to finish eating and catch up; he insisted on doing the dishes since he was a last minute guest, then left the two friends to their girl time.

Though there was no mistaking, to Farrow at least, how much he wanted to stay.

"I know that look." Bree eyed her friend, tapped lightly on her temple. "There's a lot going on up there."

"There is." But as she'd told Ryder, no decisions would be made tonight. "What do you say we open the wine Ryder brought and reminisce about our softball days?"

Bree grinned. "I say that sounds perfect, except we should put on *A League of Their Own* as inspiration."

Perfect, indeed. "Deal."

⦿⦿⦿⦿⦿

As he pulled out his glove to warm up, Levi wanted to ask Ryder if he'd talked to Farrow that day. She hadn't been at the inn when he and Jackson finalized plans with Bree—apparently she'd had obligations at the Pemberley offices—but it nagged at him that she might still disapprove of her friend's choice.

Bree didn't seem to have any doubts though, and that was what mattered. Plus, there were the looks she'd kept throwing at Jackson. It would be interesting to see how that played out.

Surely Ry had talked to his cousin, tried to persuade her to give the team a chance. But Ryder hadn't said anything, and they hadn't heard from Farrow, so now it was starting to hit him they might have to consider what to do if she said no.

That possibility was always in the back of his mind, but deep down he really thought she'd say yes.

Why did he think that? He barely knew her.

He tried to shrug it off as he and Ryder headed out to the field. He hadn't realized he was quieter than usual until Ryder asked him if he was alright.

"Yeah," Levi grunted, dragging himself out of his thoughts. "Just thinking about our catcher situation."

"Ah." Ryder seemed about to say something more, when

35

something over Levi's shoulder caught his attention, and caused a massive grin to take over his face.

Levi turned as the sound of tires over gravel reached his ears, and his eyes finally registered that it was Farrow's car. She stepped out, dressed in a pair of softball shorts and a t-shirt, hair braided back under a worn ball cap, and to his surprise, Bree stepped out of the passenger side.

Farrow waved as she pulled out her gear bag, and Levi's hand twitched in response even as he realized she was probably waving to Ryder, who was already heading back to the dugout.

Levi followed his lead, as did the rest of the team, gathering on the infield to welcome the newcomers.

Farrow met Ryder's grin with a level gaze.

"I assume by your practice-appropriate attire that you'll do it?" Ryder folded his arms expectantly and returned her gaze.

She gave one brisk nod. "Yes. I'll join the team."

"And you?" Ryder asked Bree.

"Oh, I'm just here for moral support." Bree beamed at them. "Just think of me as the team cheerleader. Which reminds me, what's the team name?"

"Yes, I also neglected to ask the team name." Farrow finally smiled, and her eyes, clear and steady, rested on Levi.

He ignored the little kick his heart gave his chest, and mustered up a mischievous grin before he answered.

"We're the Longhorns."

THREE

THE NEXT WEEK was relatively routine for Levi, in terms of baseball and work. What wasn't particularly routine, and possibly disruptive to that routine, was the omnipresence of Farrow in his days, and in his mind.

Since his family was working for Bree, and by extension her, and she was now on the team, it was nearly impossible to avoid her.

Not that he had any real reason to avoid her. He just... couldn't get his head on straight around her. It unsettled him.

Thankfully, his mismatched feelings didn't interfere with his game—he refused to let it. He could (begrudgingly) admit there were a few moments where he lost his stride during their first practice, but once he focused more on the game than the people playing it, it was simple to slide back into his flow.

Farrow continued (again, begrudgingly) to amaze him with her own skill. Not that she didn't have flaws—such as a tendency to swing at high-and-outside pitches. But behind the plate, she earned her nickname time and again, a machine attuned to all of Ryder's quirks and rhythms. It was a fun surprise to learn she could switch-hit, though she admitted she was rusty in that area.

On the field, he allowed himself to feel each aspect of his admiration for her; after all, it only served to strengthen teamwork to get along with his teammates. Off the field, though, he was inclined to suppress any hint of it, and often decided teasing her was the best outlet for those emotions.

This day was no different. It was demo day, one of the best parts of any project, other than the satisfaction of seeing it all come together. All of Bennet Family Contractors were onsite, as they would be for the rest of the project.

It had taken a few days for Bree and Farrow to go through all the rooms and clear out items and furniture, often using him and Jackson to help move things up to the attic. The exception was when things were moved into the innkeeper's apartment, which Bree and Farrow were using as a makeshift office.

He couldn't tell what Farrow thought, but he gave her credit for not seeming to mind.

With the rooms cleared and the plans finalized, it was time to tackle the intentional destruction—starting with the kitchen.

They'd just loaded in all their equipment when Bree and Farrow came down, dressed practically in jeans, work boots, and t-shirts; Bree had her hair twisted into its usual messy bun, while Farrow had secured her curls back in a braid.

Noticing the women—who would be impossible not to notice, if he were honest—and taking in their appearance, their youngest brother, Landon, offered them his most charming smile.

"Joining us, ladies?"

"Heck yeah." Bree rolled up her sleeve and flexed her bicep. "I can't wait to take a sledgehammer to this kitchen."

Farrow's face lit in an amused smirk, which Landon took as agreement.

"Awesome, the more the merrier." He clapped his hands together, a little too gleefully to Levi's mind.

Jackson, being the one with the best manners, stepped over to greet them, and proceeded to introduce Landon and the rest of the family: Their dad, Tom, whom Bree had already met, their middle brother, Mason, and their next-youngest brother, Kyle.

Levi greeted them as he handed them each some safety goggles and gloves. He shouldn't have been surprised they wanted in on demo—a lot of clients did, and they in particular seemed pretty hands on.

Maybe it was just that he hadn't prepared himself to see Farrow for longer than a perfunctory morning check-in.

Good thing he could take out his frustration with physical labor.

They'd already moved out the appliances, which were awaiting pickup from a restoration company that wanted them. The plan now was to carefully extract the cabinets, including the island, for restoration, and knock out the pointless half wall that divided the kitchen from a small dining area. They'd expand the countertop there instead, creating an L-shaped breakfast nook.

Mason, the very precise perfectionist, would do the restoration, and paint them once Bree decided on a color. They'd replace the cruddy linoleum countertop and chipped backsplash, and tear up the ugly brown tile on the floor.

Levi hadn't said anything in order not to get Bree's hopes up, but he himself was hoping they'd find the original flooring underneath.

While he and the others got to work pulling out the countertop and working on the cabinets, Jackson started in on the half-wall, demonstrating for Bree and Farrow before allowing them to join in. Much of the work went as smoothly as it could, though a few of the cabinets gave them some trouble. Once those were out and other debris was in the dumpster, the two women chipped away at the backsplash with pry bars and hammers while the rest of them hacked away at the floor.

It wasn't long before before Levi and Landon discovered a layer of sub-flooring in their section; exchanging an anticipatory grin with his brother, Levi jimmied his crow bar underneath and ripped up a corner.

"Aw, yes!" Landon exclaimed.

The others paused their work to glance over at them as they gripped the sub floor and pulled up more of it, revealing just what Levi had hoped for.

"Is that the original hardwood?" Farrow asked as Bree picked her way through the rubble to their corner.

"You bet your ass it is," Bree beamed, bending down to examine the floor. "I was hoping we'd find something cool like this. Why would anyone cover this up? It's gorgeous. Some buffing up and it'll be good as new, assuming none of it's rotted."

Mr. Bennet grunted. "Whoever remodeled this kitchen last must've cared more about the latest home design trend than the character and integrity of this home."

"We'll fix that," Bree assured him, then grinned. "What do you wanna bet we'll find more of this when we rip up that grody carpet in the dining room?"

⟨⟨⟨⟨⟨⟩⟩⟩⟩⟩

FARROW SCANNED the field as she hooked her gear bag on the dugout fence, unable to settle her nerves.

They'd been practicing for a couple weeks, and other than the snide remarks and reluctant cooperation of Billy, the team gelled well together.

Centerfielder Jackson—and Levi if she was being honest—both treated her as if she'd always been part of the team. She'd also clicked easily with their first baseman, Henry North, a guy with an easygoing and chipper attitude, and a wicked wit and sense of humor, right off the bat. Neither had it taken her long to earn the respect of their third baseman, Leo Knight, a kind and contemplative guy who lived up to his name by being both

40

strong and chivalrous—she soon learned why he was the team's main power hitter.

Their right and left fielders, Brandon Coleman and Fred Rakowski, were like two sides of the same coin. One was quiet but warm in demeanor, the other a little aloof, but not unkind; both had a certain reservedness to them. And their alternate players, Eddie Fernandez and Manny Bertolli, were both somewhat shy, but cheerful, and welcomed her with open arms.

All in all, she was confident the Longhorns could win, and now they'd have the chance to prove it.

But it wasn't the team she was worried about.

It was the Longhorns' first game of the season, sure, but it was also her first game in a few years. She hadn't mentioned this factoid to anyone on the team; only Bree, Ryder, and Andrew knew, and knew why.

And knowing, Ry sidled up next to her, nudged her none too subtly with his elbow as they both looked out over the field.

"Stop that," he suggested.

"Stop what?" But she knew.

"Thinking too much."

She nodded, swallowing the jumble of words caught in her throat. She knew he understood when he said nothing more.

She did her best to hide her distress as the rest of the team arrived, ignoring the curious stares of the other team and crowd members alike; the last thing she wanted was the attention and scrutiny of others. But she fidgeted, tugging nervously at her pristine new jersey—maroon in color, with cream-white accents and a small longhorn head on one side of the chest. And her face must have given her away; pretty much everyone but Ryder and Andrew gave her a wide berth.

The other exception was Levi, who was unabashedly looking her over as she clipped on her gear over her baseball pants.

"What?" she snapped.

Unaffected, he simply held her gaze, and the back of her neck prickled at the thought he could see right through her.

"You got this," he said softly, only loud enough for her to hear, before turning to grab up his glove.

His words settled over her like sunlight, effectively melting her icy nerves.

She further found her groove once she began to warm up with Ryder, and settled back on her haunches with satisfaction as the game began, welcoming the familiar energy.

When Ryder struck out the first batter, Bree cheered wildly from the stands, causing Ryder to blush and Farrow to grin. The second batter managed, though a little late, to connect, sending a grounder to first, where Henry scooped it up and stepped on the bag; this time Bree was joined in her cheers by Henry's girl-friend Cat Morales, who was just as enthusiastic. Similarly, their injured catcher, Frank Chopra, whom she'd met briefly, had made it out to cheer them on.

Less enthusiastic, but just as active in cheering on the team, was Levi's friend Cristina. She was a cool customer, Farrow thought—not to mention gorgeous with her sultry voice, caramel skin, button nose, and sleek, coal-black hair. The two were obviously close, which had caused an undesirable twist of envy in Farrow's gut the first time she'd seen the two of them interact. Though she liked Cristina, she couldn't tamp down the spurt of pleasure when she'd realized how clueless Levi was. Even now, his focus, as it should be, was entirely on the game.

The third batter struck out looking.

The game continued on this way for a few innings as each team took the other's measure. The opposing team snuck in a few hits once they'd gotten a handle on the Torch's pitches, and had scored a couple runs by the end of the game. But the Long-horns came out on top four-two, thanks in part to a double by Knight.

She was sure some guys on the other team resented that she was a woman, but none of them went so far as to voice that resentment. They'd all exchanged good game high-fives with her going down the line in the post-game show of sportsmanship.

All in all, a good start to the season, she mused as she packed up the catcher's gear. She caught Ryder's eye, and the smug look on his face that said *told you so*—to which she rolled her eyes.

In echo of that, a voice behind her interrupted her thoughts.

"Told you you had it."

She turned to see Levi stowing his glove in his bag, dark eyes assessing her in a way that made her feel naked.

Why did that thrill her just a little?

She zipped up the catcher's gear bag and offered him an acknowledging smile. "Indeed you did. Are your predictions always so accurate?"

His face lit with a little mischief at her teasing. "I do try not to be wrong if I can help it."

"And would you admit it if you were wrong?"

"Would you?"

There was that something else behind his eyes again, the sort of challenge. Unsure now whether he was teasing her or not, she tilted her head in a show of confusion. "Of course."

She couldn't tell if this answer satisfied him. He opened his mouth, but his response was derailed when Cristina stepped up next to him.

"Hey, great game you guys." Though she addressed both of them, her affectionate smile was all for Levi.

Oblivious, Levi grinned back at her. His affection for Cristina was clear, but, Farrow noted, it didn't hit the same note. "I really think we can win the whole thing this year, you know?"

"I agree." Though she meant it, Farrow spoke mostly to remind them of her presence and keep the situation from getting awkward. She slung her gear bag over her shoulder. "I should get going. See you at practice, Levi."

"Yeah," he said, and when he turned to zip his own bag closed, Farrow gave Cristina an understanding smile, and a nod.

Though Cristina blinked, she nodded back.

As Farrow left the dugout, Levi frowned after her. She could've at least tried to talk to Tina. Instead she'd practically ignored her, and was now interrupting whatever conversation Bree was having with Jackson and Ryder.

He could see the disappointment on his brother's face as they headed toward Farrow's car.

"Levi."

"What? Sorry." He returned his attention to Tina. "I got distracted thinking it was kind of rude of Farrow to leave just as you came over."

"I think she could tell I wanted to talk to you."

He honed in on the hesitation in her voice. "What's up?"

She paused, searching his face for something, though he didn't know what. Eventually, she took a breath before blurting, "Billy asked me out."

A blanch took over his face. "What?" When she didn't respond, he continued, "You didn't say yes, did you?"

"I told him I'd think about it. Do you care if I say yes?"

There was that searching look again, and suspicion began to seep into his brain like a shadow. "Of course I care. Billy's... Billy is...Look, you could do a whole lot better than Billy Collins. He's kind of a dick."

She was quiet again, glancing around to make sure no one else was around, clearly trying to choose her words carefully.

"Is that the only reason you care?" she finally asked. Her voice was so quiet, and she couldn't meet his eyes. And just like that, suspicion became knowing.

His stomach sank; it felt like an elevator had fallen and crashed in his gut, causing the rest of his limbs to short-circuit. This couldn't be happening.

"Tina, I..."

When he trailed off, she finally looked up, and couldn't hide the hurt on her face. It killed him, but what was he supposed to tell her? He couldn't make himself feel the same.

"How long?" he found himself asking, in a voice that sounded hollow to his own ears.

She looked away again. "A few years now."

Jesus, a few years? And he'd never freaking noticed? Some best friend he was.

Proving her own best friend abilities, she seemed to read his thoughts.

"I hid my feelings because I didn't want to ruin our friendship. I didn't want you to notice. And I guess I was hoping I'd grow out of it. I'm telling you now because…well, I'm tired of hiding it." She half-laughed, but there was no humor in it. "Takes too much energy."

His throat was dry. He hoped like hell he wasn't about to lose his best friend. "I'm sorry." A lame consolation, but it was all he had.

"Me too." Tears welled in her eyes, but she held them back. That was his Tina, always so stoic.

No. No, not his Tina anymore.

She sniffed a little, her clear brown eyes glazed with the shine of reluctant tears. "There's not even a little chance?"

His throat burned with the threat of his own tears. Was there anything he could say that wouldn't sound placating? He swallowed down the burn.

"I love you Tina, I just…" Crap, that definitely sounded placating. He looked at her, willing her to understand.

And she did. "You just love me as a friend," she finished for him, a single tear finally spilling over her cheek.

He couldn't help reaching out, brushing the tear away with his thumb. When it seemed like she was going to sob, he just pulled her in, crushed her to him. Her arms came around him, squeezed him just as hard, likely to stem her tears. She wouldn't want anyone to see her crying.

He felt her breathe deeply before releasing her hold, and he brushed his lips over her hair as he pulled back.

"I'll be alright," she told him.

It was probably dumb of him, but he had to ask. "You're not thinking of going out with Billy now, are you?"

The look she leveled at him could have turned him to stone. "If you have no intention of asking me out yourself, you have no right to tell me I can't date someone. I can't moon over you forever, Levi."

"I know," he said quickly. "I just really don't think you'd like Billy."

Her gaze softened a little. "He is kind of smarmy," she admitted, then muttered under her breath, "*Y un pendejo.*"

His lips quirked, but he couldn't smile.

"Well," Tina sighed, then gave him a discerning look. "All's fair in love and baseball. I guess I'm not that surprised, considering how obsessed you are with Farrow."

"What?" That threw him off. "I'm not obsessed with Farrow."

She shook her head at him, a little exasperated. "Levi, do you even realize how much you've asked Ryder about her over the years? How often you look at her when you think no one's watching, or how often she looks at you?"

"There's nothing going on between me and Farrow," he insisted, even as a part of his mind rebelled against the idea— and another part of him admitted he probably was a little obsessed with her.

Tina's smile was sad, and if he wasn't mistaken, pitying. "Maybe not yet."

Leaving it at that, she stepped away, leaving him alone in the dugout to try to wrap his brain around everything that just happened, and that one last little nugget of wisdom.

⭕⭕⭕⭕⭕

FOR THE NEXT SEVERAL DAYS, Levi went through the motions.

He put on a cheerful face and showed up to work at the inn, but volunteered for the tasks that would have him working alone for a bit. If his family noticed anything off, they refrained from asking him about it, for which he was grateful.

He could tell Jackson was worried about him, though, so he redoubled his efforts to be in good humor at work, and whenever Jackson was home.

He thought about texting Tina so many times, starting to type out messages before deleting them. He missed her, but what could he say?

How were they supposed to move past this?

Sometimes he wished he could return her feelings, sometimes he wished she didn't have feelings for him, and sometimes he even thought it was little selfish of her to have told him of her feelings. He understood why she had, but now they were his burden, and he was ashamed to think it. She wasn't really responsible for his feelings, any more than he was for hers.

Mostly he just wanted things to go back to the way they were. Her absence was a phantom limb in his life.

He felt it most keenly when he saw her at the coffeeshop they both frequented, sitting across from Billy on what he assumed was a date.

His feet refused to move when he saw her, and as if she sensed him, she looked up and met his eyes. She and Billy were at a table tucked in a corner, and Billy's back was to him, but even from his spot in line Levi was close enough to hear what Billy was saying. He was droning on about the level of skill he brought to the Longhorns, and Tina nodded politely as he spoke, her eyes still on Levi.

There was no way she was enjoying the conversation, Levi thought. But she'd chosen to be there, despite his own assurance that she deserved better. It hurt, just as much as the sudden estrangement between them, that she thought so little of herself as to settle for someone like Billy, even for one date.

Of course, he had no way of knowing how many dates they'd been on, and he had no right to ask.

It was she who looked away first. His heart sagged miserably, and he was tempted to just leave the shop without having ordered anything. But he forced himself to get his coffee. Made a point to let her know he wasn't going to run away.

The only thing that made him feel better was baseball.

It was the best outlet for all his conflicting emotions, and he absolutely would not let the situation with Tina put him in a slump. If anything, it fueled him. For a couple hours, at least, he could escape thinking about his problems.

Some of his teammates noticed the intensity of his focus; he could often feel Jackson and Ryder watching him carefully, as they knew him well, and were probably right to be concerned. But he also felt another pair of eyes on him with alarming discernment.

Farrow stared at him as much as she ever had, but he could tell there was something else behind the looks she gave him. Instead of glancing away when he caught her looking, she started tilting her head, or raising a brow. Her way of checking in, he supposed. She never outright asked him if he was okay, and maybe he was imagining it, but he couldn't help wondering if she knew what occurred with Tina, and just how it was affecting him.

Regardless, the unexpected show of support was a surprising source of comfort.

They'd had a couple games during the week, both of which they'd won, thanks to some stellar pitching from Ryder, and an epic home run from Knight.

They also had a small cheer section, which consisted of Bree, and Henry's adorably excitable girlfriend, Cat. They declared their intention to show up for every game, and enthusiastically pumped up their team, while taunting their opponents with punny jeers such as, "You've been pitch slapped!" which they said whenever Ryder struck someone out looking.

It always made Levi smile.

They were even gifted their own Longhorns jerseys and ball caps by the team, with their last names printed on the back, just like the rest of the team.

Frank didn't make it to every game, but came when he was able, keen to root for his team even if he couldn't play.

One person who stayed away was Tina. Part of him was relieved—he'd been worried seeing her would be distracting—but on the other hand, it stung. Even if she'd wanted to be there to cheer on Jackson and Ryder, and now Billy, evidently she stayed away for his sake. Jackson and Ryder definitely noticed she wasn't there, but if they suspected her reasons, they didn't say.

Now it was Saturday, and they had an afternoon game against the Redcoats.

He and Jackson warmed up together, since Ryder usually warmed up with Farrow now. He was so focused on the back and forth of catch he didn't notice Billy was late. It wasn't until five minutes before the game was set to start that Billy showed up, stomping his way into the dugout and knocking shoulders with Levi on his way to hang his gear bag.

Levi opened his mouth to say something, but felt a hand on his arm. He turned to see Farrow watching him, shin guards already strapped to her legs.

"Ignore him. He's clearly in a mood."

He nodded, and because she was still touching him, he could feel it when she went rigid, and he was close enough to hear her sharp intake of breath.

"What?" he asked, automatically searching for something wrong. But all he saw was the other team getting ready to bat. "Farrow?"

She only kept staring at the other team. Gripping her arm, he turned her to face him. "What's wrong?"

"Something's wrong?" Wondering why Ro wasn't putting the rest of her catcher's gear on, Ryder had approached her and

Levi, only to be alarmed by the stricken look on his cousin's face.

She leveled her gaze at him, voice steely when she said, "Look who's on the other team."

Ryder narrowed his eyes, looking across the infield to scan the players—and his eyes alighted on a face he'd very much like to meet his fist. "Shit."

"What?" Impatient now, Levi had dropped Farrow's arm and glanced between the cousins in confusion.

"See the blonde guy? With the neon yellow cleats?" Ryder murmured. "His name is Greg Wyatt. Ro and I have an unsavory history with him."

"Is he really good or something?"

"No," Farrow answered, and she said it so matter-of-factly Levi almost missed the bite behind the word. Then she turned abruptly and went to finish putting on her gear.

Levi looked to Ryder for an explanation, but Ry only shook his head. There wasn't enough time; and besides, it was Ro's story more than his. "A story for another time."

But Levi noticed Ryder gathered Andrew, who'd been speaking to Billy, and they both went over to speak to Farrow, distinct frowns occupying all their faces.

When they took their places on the field, Levi noticed Farrow had twisted her hair into a low bun, allowing her backward ball cap and the catcher's mask to hide her hair. He didn't think anything of it until Ryder started throwing a few warm up pitches; Levi happened to glance at the Redcoats' dugout, and saw Wyatt's gaze honed in on the pitcher's mound, something cold about his expression.

But he barely glanced behind the plate, and Levi realized with her long hair hidden, and all the catcher's gear on, Farrow wouldn't look like a woman to anyone not paying much attention. She'd never gone to any lengths to hide herself before, and it worried him she did so now. Who was this Wyatt guy?

Despite the strange start to the game, the first inning went well. Three up, three down for them on the field—two strike outs and one play at first. When it was their turn to bat, Henry surprised the other team by leading off with a double.

The wild cheering at Henry's hit had Levi glancing at the stands, unsurprised to see Bree clapping and Cat jumping up and down. But his breath hitched when he saw that Tina was sitting with them, cheering just as loudly, and sporting a Longhorns jersey of her own. She looked in his direction, and when she tipped her head in a subtle nod, his speeding heart settled.

They would need to talk, but he hadn't lost his best friend.

After that, his attention was fully on the game, and by the end of the inning the Longhorns were up one-nothing. Everything was fine until the third inning, when Farrow had to finally take the chest protector off to bat.

Some of the other players, especially a loud-mouthed prick, called Thorpe by his team, made noises about a woman being allowed to play. They had to pause the game while Andrew assured their captain—a guy named Denny—their coach, and the ump they had the league's full permission.

But it really started going downhill once Wyatt finally noticed *Darcy* emblazoned on the back of Farrow's jersey.

She managed to hit a single into left field in her first at bat, despite the leering of the opposing team. But she was thrown out at second when Manny, their next batter, hit a grounder to short. They didn't get any runs that inning, but neither did the Redcoats; Farrow was, if anything, extra focused on her catching, and the Dynamic Duo certainly proved their worth. By the end of the eighth inning, the Longhorns were up three to two, thanks largely to some more powerful hits from Brandon and Eddie.

Unfortunately, going into the top of the ninth, the Redcoats' big hitters were next in the line up. The one they called Crawford swaggered to the plate, and after fouling a couple, smacked the ball far enough into left field to earn himself a double. He made it to third when Thorpe hit a grounder to second, which Billy scooped up and threw to Henry at first.

The next hitter, a pleasant-faced charmer with Willoughby spelled across the back of his broad shoulders, tried to hit on Farrow. When she ignored him, he only shrugged, smiling smugly before swinging at the next pitch, and sending it into left field shallowly enough that Fred couldn't get there in time. Willoughby ran safely to first, while Crawford made a beeline for home.

The score was tied.

Levi groaned when Forster, a tall S.O.B. with tree trunks for legs approached the plate next; he'd been responsible for the hit that brought in the Redcoats' previous two runs. And he proved his power again by smashing it over the right field fence.

Willoughby practically danced around the bases, while Forster jogged behind him.

Wyatt was next, sauntering to the batter's box almost lazily. He ignored Farrow and glared down Ryder, swinging at the first pitch. He sent a line drive whizzing right to Levi, who barely had to take a step to snag it. And the next batter, Elton, struck out swinging.

They had one more at-bat to retake the lead, and though Farrow thought they could do it, a part of her just wanted the game to be over. As she took a drink from her water bottle, she noticed Wyatt putting catcher's gear on instead of staying in right field.

Great. Just what she needed.

Ryder led off the inning, edging out a single after working his way up to a full count. He was followed by Brandon, who cracked it into center field, where the fly was caught by that giant Forster guy. Jackson was next, and his patience rewarded him with a walk; with two on base and only one out, they still had a good chance, and Farrow stepped out on deck for some practice swings.

Their good chance became less good when Fred nicked a

grounder right to the third baseman, who only had to step on third to tag Ryder out.

Farrow's nerves scrambled under her skin; she felt chilled and clammy at the same time, and so took a breath before stepping into the batter's box. She deliberately reminded herself to stay loose as she settled into her stance.

"How's Gemma?"

The question had been murmured low enough the ump didn't hear, just as she took a step to swing; it proved enough to distract her, and she swung just a little too late, sending the ball skittering down the first base line out of play.

"Does she miss me?" Wyatt whispered as the ball was returned to the pitcher.

She ignored him, and the next pitch. But thoughts of her sister were still distracting. On the next pitch she fouled the ball right into the fence behind home.

"C'mon, Vac!" Bree called from the stands, then began chanting a cheer from their softball days she thought of as the "Olé" cheer. *"Olé, olé, olé olé. Hit the ball the other way. Our team is hot, hot, hot, your team is not, not, not; so hit the ball, ball, ball, over the wall, wall, wall."*

Bree's encouragement nearly settled her, but Wyatt had one last taunt up his sleeve.

"Did you know her chapstick tastes like pomegranate?"

The comment stopped her cold, and her arms felt like noodles as they belatedly got the message to swing the bat, hit nothing but air.

Strike three.

"Guess that's game over." Wyatt smirked as he stood. "Better luck next time."

FOUR

SHE WAS NO LONGER CLAMMY—JUST chilled. Goosebumps prickled on her arms despite the thick, stifling humidity. She kept her anger at a simmer, deliberately removing her batting helmet with care, quietly stowing it in their team bag of helmets.

"Ro."

"Not now," she said to Ryder.

He shook his head, his eyes zeroed in on her. "What did he say to you?"

"Not now," she repeated in the same bland tone. "I need to be alone."

He continued to look at her as she began to put away the rest of her gear. He didn't look happy, but eventually he nodded. "Later, then."

"Later," she agreed.

As if they could sense human contact might set her off, the rest of the team kept their distance from her. Once Andrew gave them all a "See you Monday," she walked to her car without looking back.

Levi watched her go, resisting the sudden urge to go after her. But he'd heard her tell Ryder she wanted to be alone.

And as he made it back to his own car, he saw that Cristina was there, leaning against the driver's side door.

He stopped near the hood, swallowed. "Hi."

"Hi." Then her lips curved, and she pushed off the door. He dropped his gear bag and opened his arms as she stepped into them, enfolding her tight against him.

"I missed you," he murmured against her hair.

"I missed you, too." She gave him one more squeeze before pulling back. "Coffee?"

He shook his head. "I need a beer. And food."

"Even better."

He went home to change real quick, then met her at a burger joint they both favored, and they were mostly silent until they ordered. Once they had, Tina set her elbows on the table and asked him what he'd been up to the past week. He caught her up on the inn project, and the games she'd missed, at which point their server dropped off their beers. When he had nothing more to say, he leaned forward, looked at her. Waited.

"I broke it off with Billy," she started. "That time you saw us in the coffee shop was our only actual date, but I'm not sure that qualifies either. He just kind of...talked at me the whole time. And I don't think he ever once asked me about myself, the entire week."

She smiled weakly. "Obviously, you were right. He is kind of a dick."

"And an asshole," he reminded her, lips twitching.

"*Y un pendejo*," she conceded, and her expression turned distant. "It didn't take me long to realize going out with him because you'd rejected me was just stupid. I had no interest in him at all, and when he asked when our second date would be, I told him there wouldn't be one."

Now her eyes flicked back to his, and she kept her gaze direct. It was something she did whenever she felt she was saying something truly important, so he inclined his head to make sure she knew she had his full attention.

"The thing is…" She took a breath. "Somewhere during this whole escapade, I realized that as much as I missed you, I wasn't *longing* for you. Not the way I thought I had been."

He blinked. "What do you mean?"

"I mean I think I conflated my feelings for you," she explained. "A few years ago, when Ryder started talking about Farrow, and you were so intrigued by her, I was jealous. I assumed that meant I must have romantic feelings for you, and maybe on some level I did. But I think it was mostly just convenient for me; I wanted to be in love with someone—and who better than my best friend? So, I convinced myself I was in love with you, and the more interested you were in Ryder's mentions of Farrow, the easier it was."

He listened with a sense of disbelief, and he was sure she could see his skepticism in the furrowing of his brows. "So that's it? You were just mistaken? You've magically realized you were never in love with me?"

"I know it sounds hard to believe."

"That's because it is." He sighed, watching her carefully. "Tina, as much as I want our friendship to go back to the way it was, I also don't want you to say all this just to make me feel better."

"I'm not."

"How do you know?"

"Because." She cleared her throat, blushing a little. "Even though you're very attractive…"

At this he raised a brow, and she glanced down at her hands, but forged ahead. "And I did go so far as to fantasize kissing you, I never once imagined…anything more. I tried, but something stopped me every time."

She bit her lip, cheeks pinking further, and took a sip of her drink to avoid looking at him. He thought he understood, and his lips quirked into an amused smile.

"So I'm hot enough to kiss, but not have sex with?"

Tina sputtered. "Levi!"

It was good to hear her laugh, he thought. Good that they could laugh about it.

"If that's the way you want to put it," she teased, "Yes, I could probably stand kissing you, but I can't imagine being intimate with you."

"Same," he admitted.

Her eyebrows perked up. "What do you mean, 'same?'"

"I may have thought about kissing you once or twice, when we were in high school." He shrugged. "Even debated trying it, but then David Carter asked you out and I didn't mind at all."

Her eyes had widened at his confession, but now she smiled readily as she thought back to their teen years. "That was junior year. And after I started dating David, you started dating Nora Dashwood."

"Yep." He had fond memories of Nora. She'd been a very sweet and wicked smart girl with a talent for sketching, and they'd dated until the summer before college, when they amicably decided to part ways. "I saw on Instagram that she's just moved back from L.A."

"Really? I thought she had a job at a film studio."

"She took a job at an independent animation studio downtown. We'll have to catch up with her."

"Absolutely," Tina grinned, and a particular glint came into her eyes when she suggested, "We could invite her to a game."

"We could." Levi was almost afraid to ask what that glint was about. If she had some scheme in mind, he didn't want to know.

And just as the lull in their conversation came, so did their food, for which Levi's empty stomach was eternally grateful.

⁂

THOUGH HIS REUNION with Tina had significantly boosted his mood, once he was alone, Levi's thoughts automatically drifted to Farrow, and their first loss of the season.

It happened, he thought as he drove toward home. They couldn't be expected to win every game.

But there was something troubling about Farrow's reaction to Greg Wyatt, not to mention Ryder's and Andrew's reactions. Ryder had indicated their history with Wyatt was less than stellar, but what concerned Levi was the effect he clearly had on Farrow.

And he'd obviously said something to her that had, at the very least, gotten under her skin. Levi could admit now what he hadn't been able to earlier: he was worried about her.

As he approached the baseball fields, he was surprised to see their usual practice field wasn't empty. He could make out a lone figure stalking toward home plate, a bat on their shoulder. Curious, he turned into the park entrance; even before he parked next to her car, he recognized Farrow, dressed much like she'd been at that first practice in jeans, her orange converse, and her Longhorns jersey, dropping a small bundle of baseballs on the other side of the plate.

It felt as though thinking of her had summoned him there. Keeping his eyes on her, he stepped out of the car; surely she'd noticed him drive up, heard the door slam shut, but she studiously ignored anything but the bat and ball in her hand. He was close enough now to see her face, set in frustration and grim determination.

He walked toward the dugout, watching her eyes narrow in concentration, as she held the ball out in front of her, her bat gripped in the other hand; then she bent her legs, lowered her arm, and tossed the ball straight up into the air over the plate. When it descended back into range, she swung, sending the ball into the outfield with a piercing *crack!*

Then she picked up another ball, did the same thing, only this time she swung harder. He watched her fungo the remaining couple balls in quick succession, drop her bat, and stomp out to collect the balls.

How long had she been out here? Did she realize it was nearly sunset?

He thought for a moment she seemed angry, but decided anger was too simple an emotion for her present disposition; her every move was stilted and hard, like she was just managing to contain a barely suppressed rage.

He had a feeling he knew what had caused such rage, though he doubted she wanted to talk about it.

By the time she returned to the batter's box, he'd gone to retrieve his mitt, and was standing in front of home plate, arms crossed and brow raised.

"Levi." She acknowledged him with a nod, her tone one of affected indifference.

He didn't buy it for a second. He could practically see the storm cloud above her head, bruise gray and crackling with furious, untamed energy.

Well, he could act as a lightning rod, he supposed.

"Need a hand?" he asked.

"No."

"You sure? I can go field anything you hit, or I can try pitching for you."

Eyeing him, she dropped her arms, letting the balls plop unceremoniously in the dirt, then placed her hands on her hips.

"Why are you here?" she bit out.

He kept his tone and smile even as he picked up one of the balls that had rolled against his foot. "I was curious who was practicing by themselves at this hour. You?"

When she said nothing, he casually tossed the ball up, let it fall lightly into his glove.

"Because it seems to me," he said just as casually, eyes on the ball's trajectory as he lobbed it up and caught it again, "that you're trying to blow off some steam. I can help with that."

This time when he tossed up the ball, she stepped over and snatched it out of the air before it could land in his glove. He only lifted his brows, waiting for her to speak.

"I'm not very good company right now," she said plainly.

"I'm not here for company." He paused and met her eyes as it occurred to him why he'd joined her. "I'm here because you're upset, and I want to help."

"I don't want to talk about it."

He shook his head. "No talking necessary. Just swinging at balls. You can pretend they're Wyatt's."

This got a sliver of a smirk, and a quiet huff that informed him his hunch was correct. She watched him carefully for a moment before finally sighing, nodding at him.

"Fine. You can pitch."

He scooped up the balls and carried them to the mound, setting them to the side. He did his best to throw accurately, preferring that over trying to throw it hard and fast. They weren't great pitches, but they weren't terrible either; besides, he wasn't trying to be good at it—she just needed something to hit.

She hit a grounder first, then let the next pitch sail by and bounce off the back fence before lobbing it back at his feet. She hit the next two a little harder, just past the edge of the infield, and missed the last one.

He gestured for her to stay put as he went to collect the ones she'd hit, and they repeated the process; this time her hits were more consistent, and she nearly took his head off with a hard line drive that smacked into his glove inches from his face.

"Whew." Chuckling, he blew out a breath.

"Sorry." Her expression went from concentrated anger to sheepish in a heartbeat.

"You're fine," he assured her, and gestured for her to keep going.

She hesitated, but nodded, and by the loosening of her stance, he guessed she was done swinging as hard as she could. Perhaps it was time to lighten the mood.

For her amusement, he played it up as she took her stance, making an exaggeratedly focused face, pretending to shake his head at an imaginary catcher's pitch suggestions before nodding, pivoting, and hiking his leg absurdly high.

She let out a short laugh, too distracted to swing in time when he let the ball fly.

"Hey!" she complained, but there was no edge to it.

He grinned, winked. "Gotta keep you on your toes."

They went through a couple more rounds this way, with him acting as a caricature of a pitcher, and her playing around with different swings, even switch-hitting a few times to test him.

He decided to mix it up by tossing it underhand, which made her laugh, even as she sent the ball flying over his head. When he threw it underhand again, she crouched low over the plate, tapping the ball in a bunt, and surprised him by taking off down the first base line.

Now it was his turn to exclaim, "Hey!"

He leapt toward the ball, which had made it about three-quarters of the way toward the mound, grabbing it up and racing after her.

She was fast, but so was he; she had a second's head start, but he had longer legs.

They made it to the bag at nearly the same time, though her head start proved enough to get her there first. He reached out his foot to tap the base just after hers, and as she turned her head to give him a wicked grin, her shoe slipped on the dirt-brushed surface of the base.

Instinctively, she yelped and reached out to grip his arm for support, even as he reached out to catch her, the result of which was they both lost their balance and went down in a heap of tangled limbs.

He landed on his butt, managing to catch himself reasonably well, while she'd twisted to land on her hip, her hands smacking the dirt with a thud.

"Oof," she mumbled. But before he could ask if she was alright, she started laughing.

It was a bright, delighted sound that shot straight to his gut and lit a fire. And it had him shaking his head and laughing along with her.

Eventually their laughter died out and left them grinning at each other, and he pushed up and pulled off his glove, held out his hands to her.

She smacked her hands against her jeans, causing little puffs of dirt to sprout around her as she dusted some of it off before clasping them in his, then pushed up with her legs. He pulled her up with minimal effort, but even so, he wasn't expecting the momentum with which she got to her feet.

She bumped into his chest, and without thinking, he placed a hand against her waist to keep her steady. In turn, her newly freed palm slapped against his chest to steady herself, eyes widening when she peered up at him and realized how close they were.

"Is the next dance a waltz?" he asked, his voice a little huskier than usual.

"Ha." She practically squeaked in response, and stepped back. "Sorry. These shoes have no traction anymore; I shouldn't have been running on the dirt."

She lifted her foot to show him the bottom of her Converse, where the tread was almost entirely smoothed.

He nodded, but smiled. "I'm not exactly wearing field-appropriate shoes either. But maybe we should call it a night."

"Probably."

But she didn't move, and neither did he. She had an odd little smile on her face, studying him patiently, and he wasn't sure if she was waiting for him to speak or not. When the silence stretched a bit too long, she bit her lip.

"You've got…" She tapped a finger against her chest, and he looked down at his own chest to see a light handprint dusted on his shirt where her hand had been.

"Oh." He brushed it away with a few swipes before glancing back over at her.

She was still chewing on her lip, watching and waiting as if she expected him to do or say something else—but her lips still curved slightly in that quiet smile.

Yeah, it was awkward, he thought. But it was a wonderfully far cry from the weary, rage-filled Farrow he'd come across.

He finally realized the sun had nearly disappeared now, said, "I'll help you pack up," and headed to the grass to retrieve the balls she'd hit out there.

When he got back to the dugout, she'd already slipped her bat back in its slot in her gear bag and slipped the remaining ball in a side pouch. He handed her the others, unable to ignore the little zing that went through him when her fingers ghosted over his. When she'd zipped up the side pouch, she slung the bag over her shoulder.

"Shall we?" she asked.

At his nod, they walked to their cars in silence; she threw her bag in her trunk while he stowed his glove back in his, and still the silence held.

When she'd closed her trunk, she turned to him, the last dregs of golden light giving her dark hair ethereal highlights. He shoved his hands in his pockets, just to have something to do with them.

"Well, goodnight. Drive safe," he said.

"You, too."

He'd only taken a couple steps when, in a hurried, almost breathless voice, she called, "Levi?"

His steps halted, and he turned back around, raised his eyebrows expectantly. Her eyes moved in quick succession over his face as indecision wavered in them; but before he could speak, she moved toward him, stepping up to him and placing one hand on his shoulder, the other lightly against his cheek.

She raised herself up onto her tip-toes, instinctively causing him to bend his head down as she pressed her soft lips to his other cheek.

"Thank you," she murmured next to his ear, before pulling away and turning to open her car door.

"You're welcome," he said absently, even as she closed it. His feet moved mechanically toward his own car door, but his eyes continued to watch her as she drove away.

It was nothing, he told himself. Just a little peck on the cheek.

And yet, there'd been that zing again. And the feel of her pressed close to him, her breath tickling his ear...

Had she noticed goosebumps had broken out down his arms?

It'd taken everything decent in him not to tug her against him and ravish her mouth—or better yet, pull her into the backseat of his truck and see if they could steam up the windows.

Somewhere in the back of his mind, the idea he was attracted to her had hovered like a helicopter waiting to land; objectively, he'd known it was there, but now it was just plain obvious and he could no longer deny it.

Because, damn it, he cared about her.

What had finally done it? he wondered. The kiss? Her laugh?

It was a bunch of little things, he realized as his mind raced through all their interactions. And this, tonight, was the first time they'd been alone together. He'd wanted to help her vent her anger without really asking himself why, and she'd let him for reasons unknown to him.

And they'd had fun. They'd actually laughed together.

And she'd thanked him, and kissed him goodbye, and now he couldn't deny he liked her.

Wanted her.

Now what the hell was he supposed to do about that?

⟨⟨⟨⟨⟩⟩⟩⟩

SHE COULD USE A NICE, full glass of wine, Farrow thought as she shed the dirt-smudged clothes she'd hastily changed into in the back of her car after the game. And, what the hell, an indulgently long shower—she deserved it.

So thinking, she walked to the kitchen in her robe and underwear, poured herself a glass nearly to the brim before heading to the bathroom and stripping down. She took her wine with her into the shower, sipping every now and then as she took her time scrubbing the field dirt from her skin and reflecting on her impromptu practice with Levi.

She'd spent the drive home recalling how it felt to have his arms around her, and the feel of his stubble-rough cheek under her lips. Wondering what would have happened if she'd given him a proper kiss.

And now, in the comfort of home, she allowed herself to think about what it meant to her that he'd come. She didn't know how he ended up at the field, but she was glad, and grateful.

She'd seen him embracing Tina, and her heart had ached to see it—ached with both joy and sadness. Though she'd suspected Tina's feelings, she couldn't know for sure what had happened between them; her only clue was Tina's absence, which had indicated a disagreement of some kind. While she was glad to see Levi make up with his best friend, she couldn't deny she'd be disappointed if he decided he returned Tina's feelings.

But somehow he'd found her at the field, and insisted on staying with her. He might have guessed some of what was bothering her, and he'd not only wanted to comfort her, he'd also managed to make her feel better.

She'd nearly hurt him with her angry batting, which had instantly doused the fire—the need to hit something. His goofball antics had amused her, then cheered her, and the fact he'd cared enough to help her work through her anger only served to make her like him more.

And the heat she thought she'd detected in his eyes when

he'd held her gave her hope there might be something between them after all.

She was still contemplating this possibility as she put on a cozy pair of sleep shorts and a tee, and her phone buzzed from the nightstand. She thought it might be Ryder—she did have a couple texts from him—but it was Bree.

"Hey," she answered, tucking the phone under her ear as she walked to the kitchen. Her stomach was grumbling, as she'd neglected to eat, but she could scrounge up a late dinner to go with her wine. "What's up? If it's about Wyatt, I don't want to talk about him."

"No, it's not about Wyatt," came the nervous response. "I have a dilemma."

"You always have a dilemma."

"I know, but…" Bree paused. "I think…I think Jackson might ask me out."

Opening the fridge, Farrow reached for ingredients to make a sandwich. "Oh."

"Yeah."

"Why do you think that?" She set everything she wanted on the counter, then put her phone on speaker and set it on the counter, too.

"I don't know, I just realized he kind of seeks me out. He doesn't really flirt, but he does pay a lot of attention to me…and I may have paid some attention to him back."

Farrow paused. "So are you saying you want him to ask you out?"

"I don't know. I do like him."

Farrow sighed.

Bree must have heard, because she said, "You see my dilemma."

"Honestly?" Farrow paused again. "I don't. I don't understand why you're doing this to yourself."

When there was no response, she added a couple slices of

cheese to her sandwich and kept going. "You have feelings for someone else, Bree. That's not fair to you or to Jackson."

"I know, but what if—"

"And how do you think Ry would feel if you started dating someone? One of his closest friends?"

The line was quiet as Farrow finished making her sandwich.

Finally, Bree's voice came softly from the phone. "Ryder doesn't see me that way. Maybe going out with someone else will help me get over him."

"I'm pretty sure you're wrong about that." Actually, she was one hundred percent sure about that. "What if he does have feelings for you, but like you, thinks you don't feel that way about him?"

"…Do you think so?"

Farrow resisted sighing again. "Bree, if you want to find out how Ryder feels about you, you need to bite the bullet and ask him."

She couldn't see her friend, but she imagined Bree was biting her lip. "What if I ask him out, and he says no?"

"The answer will always be no if you never ask."

Which was exactly what she'd told Ryder multiple times, but he hadn't listened. For whatever reason, something held him back. Maybe Bree would listen, and she could finally stop watching two of the people she loved most torture themselves over their lovesick lack of communication.

It was Bree who sighed this time. "I'll think about it. But you're right. It would be unfair to lead Jackson on."

A little later, after they'd said goodnight, Farrow sat on her couch and polished off her sandwich as she thought about Bree and Ryder's situation. She'd put on a video from one of her favorite YouTube channels on the TV, but she barely paid any attention to it.

It had pained her over the years to see Ryder do nothing about his feelings for Bree, and her for him in turn. She'd never understood it.

But now, she thought maybe she was starting to understand. It was a bit terrifying to fall in love. Some might find it exciting, a reason to celebrate. And it was—or, at least, she thought maybe she'd get there eventually.

She'd thought maybe it was just attraction, and considered it an inconvenience. Then eventually she'd admitted there was some interest, but worked to hide it; she didn't need the distraction of dating. But something had shifted today; there on the field, she'd been vulnerable, and he'd been there for her. She could acknowledge now her heart had ached with something else entirely.

Now she wanted to feel it, and couldn't stop the smile that overtook her face at the thrill. But that didn't make it any less scary to realize she was probably falling in love with Levi Bennet.

FIVE

A FEW WEEKS LATER, Levi still hadn't figured out what to do with his feelings for Farrow.

Which sucked, because he was seeing even more of her than before. They'd had several more games, and despite his distraction, he played well; and after their loss to the Redcoats, the Longhorns hit a winning streak. Their little fan section, which now included Tina, had much to cheer about.

The only thorn in their side, as it were, was Billy.

After Tina broke it off with him, he became quietly hostile toward Levi, barely speaking to him unless it was required and not bothering to hide his disdain. He'd then tried to ask Farrow out, but after she declined, his bitterness extended to the whole team. During one game, Andrew even had to sit Billy out for its remainder, for which Billy complained no one appreciated him.

Frankly, Levi was over Billy's attitude and did his best to ignore it.

But he was done ignoring what he felt for Farrow, and every time they were remotely alone, he had to restrain himself from backing her against a wall and kissing her senseless.

Recently, the wall in question was one of the hallway nook walls where they were busy setting up the library. He and his dad had placed themselves in charge of that room, and Farrow volunteered to help; they'd gotten the window seat built, and were nearly done installing all the bookshelves.

But Mr. Bennet often stepped out to go check on the other projects, which left Levi and Farrow alone but for the clattering of other construction and chatter throughout the house.

It wasn't a bad thing, Levi mused. In fact, his mood had been significantly buoyed by those small moments with her, enough to carry him for the rest of day.

And though she seemed to enjoy it, too—though she seemed more comfortable and relaxed around him, and her smiles were more natural—he still couldn't decide if he should make a move. They'd stumbled into friendship, and the last thing he wanted to do was ruin that before they'd barely begun.

Today they would finish the library built-ins, and it would be really satisfying to see it all come together. And since he was already thinking about Farrow, he decided to distract himself by thinking about Jackson and Bree.

Levi had to admit he wasn't entirely sure what happened there. Last week, Jackson had asked Bree out; since they'd seemed to like each other a lot, he couldn't determine why Bree had turned Jackson down.

Poor Jackson still stared at her a lot, his eyes constantly drawn to the bleachers during games, or watching Bree leave a room. He kept assuring everyone he was fine, but he'd been even more reticent than usual. It didn't help that Bree was still friendly with him, which made the whole thing awkward.

"That's a really intense thinking face you've got there."

"Hm?"

He looked up to find Farrow watching him with something like amusement and no little curiosity.

"This is you," she said, and proceeded to demonstrate by turning her mouth down in a pursed frown, tipping her head to glare at the floor. Then she straightened and cleared the expression from her face. "You were thinking pretty hard over there."

"Yeah, I guess I was." His brow automatically furrowed, and he shook himself out of it.

"Careful, your brain's not an Etch-a-Sketch."

He chuckled. "Oh, that it were."

"I feel that. Do you want to talk about it?" She hesitated. "Did you argue with Cristina?"

"No, Tina and I are all good."

And they were. They'd refortified their friendship in the past few weeks, and had moved on from everything enough Tina not only felt comfortable teasing him about his crush on Farrow, but had befriended Farrow.

"I was actually thinking about Jackson and Bree," he admitted. "It seemed like they were pretty into each other, but she said no when he asked her out. Has she said anything to you?"

He hadn't really decided if he should ask Farrow about Bree, but it seemed his curiosity and concern for his brother won out over tact.

Farrow hesitated, looked away. "We've talked about it. Her feelings are private, but I will say she feels bad for leading him on. She didn't do it intentionally—she does like him. But she has other feelings that prevented her from accepting him, and I reminded her it wouldn't be fair to anyone involved."

"What does that even mean, other feelings?" His gaze narrowed, suspicion making him hone in on her face. "Are you saying you convinced her not to go out with him?"

She lifted her chin a little, eyes narrowing back. "I didn't convince her of anything. I only reminded her of her own feelings."

He gritted his teeth, struggled to keep from raising his voice. "Again, what does that mean? And what right did you have to interfere?"

"She asked for my advice," Farrow said calmly. "I gave her my honest opinion."

"Which is what, exactly?"

On a short huff of breath she closed her eyes, and pinched

the bridge of her nose. "That it would be unfair to Jackson to go out with him when she's in love with someone else."

That was the last thing he'd expected, and for a moment or two he could only stand there and blink at her. "What? Who... what?"

"And now I've told you something about my friend I doubt she would have told you herself." She sounded frustrated, but her face softened with pity and understanding. "I know it's kind of a mess. I'm sorry if Jackson's feelings were hurt."

Absently, he rubbed at his shoulder, his thoughts tumbling over each other in their haste to make their way to the front of his mind.

Bree was in love with someone else? Did Jackson know? And for Pete's sake, what was with all the love triangles recently?

"You're making the face again."

Farrow's voice snapped him out of it. When he flicked his eyes to her, she looked a little withdrawn. Wary—of him, he realized. And it dawned on him that he'd basically forced her to tell him something she and Bree had probably discussed in confidence.

"I'm...sorry for pushing you to tell me something that's none of my business."

She shrugged, the gesture loose and defeated. "It'll probably come out soon, anyway."

He shot her a questioning look, but he didn't dare ask more. And, interestingly, she smiled. A bit slyly if his expression-reading skills were still intact.

"You'll just have to wait and see," was all she said.

His blood heated a little, and he couldn't help thinking there was another circumstance under which she might give him that particular smile. Then he berated himself; it was inappropriate to be thinking dirty thoughts about her after the conversation they'd just had. They were both a bit wound up. Even if he'd been considering making a move today, this would have spoiled it.

When he had yet to respond, she tilted her head, then walked over to him. Confused, he only watched her approach, swallowed when she stopped surprisingly close to him and reached up with one hand.

She touched her finger lightly between his brows. "What's going on up there?"

The breath he was unaware he'd been holding released on a huff of laughter. "You sure know how to throw a guy some curveballs."

"I suppose I do." She didn't back away, just continued to look up at him, blue eyes twinkling just a little. "Are you telling me you don't know how to swing a bat?"

That sounded a lot like flirtation to him, and he paused to consider his response. "More like I'm still deciding when to take a swing."

Her lips curved on one side as she looked down. "Ah. Waiting for the right pitch. I know what that's like—metaphorically and literally."

He smiled a little now, buoyed by the game and the cheesy metaphors. He decided to test his chances. "Do I have any strikes?"

Her head whipped back up. He'd kept his gaze on her so there'd be no mistaking what he was referring to, and she must have gotten the message, because she gave him the same sly smile that had provoked fantasies in him just moments ago.

"You're still at bat."

He smiled back, but before either of them could say more, Mr. Bennet returned. They stepped away from each other, a bit awkwardly, but the fact his dad didn't tease them about it told Levi he hadn't paid much attention to them.

That, or he'd just tease Levi later.

Either way, it didn't matter. Unless he was reading her wrong, Farrow had just confirmed she was interested in him.

Now all he had to do was figure out what to do next.

⟨⟨⟨⟨⟨⟩

An opportunity arose the very next day, and came from a rather unexpected source.

Saturday morning, Levi awoke to the earthy aroma of coffee and the sticky-sweet scent of pancakes, and wandered into the kitchen to find Jackson at the stove. Jackson had often claimed cooking helped him think, and his blank expression as he slid a finished pancake onto a plate made Levi wonder if he was thinking about Bree.

Moving cautiously, as though he were trying not to spook a horse, Levi grabbed a mug and poured some of the coffee. He gave his brother the gimlet eye as he sipped.

"So…pancakes, huh? What's the occasion?"

"Bree's dating Ryder."

Levi sputtered a little on his next sip as hot coffee went down the wrong pipe. He had expected Jackson to hedge, and he wasn't sure what to make of the fact he'd just come right out and said it.

"I see," he managed to croak before coughing again. When his throat was clear, he asked, "How'd you find that out?"

"Ryder told me." Jackson turned off the stove, plated the last pancake. "We had a talk about it last night."

"Are you okay?"

"Actually, I am." Jackson picked up his own coffee and leaned against the counter, a small smile lighting up his face. "I know I was pretty cryptic after Bree turned me down, but she'd asked me not to say anything. Now that the cat's out of the bag, I can tell you."

"I may have poked at Farrow about it," Levi admitted sheepishly. "She told me Bree was in love with someone, but she didn't say who."

Jackson gave him as scolding a look as he was able, but

nodded. "Bree said as much to me, except she told me it was Ry. I assured her she didn't need to explain, but she was worried it would strain my friendship with him. I promised it wouldn't."

Levi picked up a pancake, still warm, and took a bite. "So you've known this for almost a couple weeks?"

Jackson nodded. "I was a little worried about Bree, since I didn't know if she'd said anything to Ryder, but I've also been using the time to think."

Several questions zipped through Levi's mind, but he didn't want to stray from the current topic. "But Ryder talked to you."

"Yeah, we met up for a beer because he wanted to talk to me." Jackson shrugged. "He confessed he'd been in love with Bree for years. And when I asked if he was going to tell her…he admitted they'd told each other how they feel a week ago."

"For real? Why the secrecy?"

"They had their reasons, but I think you should hear them from Ryder yourself."

Levi shook his head. "I have so many questions." But instead of asking them, Levi shoved the rest of the pancake in his mouth.

"Well, you'll get a chance to ask them this afternoon if you want," Jackson told him. "He got tickets to the Cubs-Cardinals game, and invited us along."

"Really?" Going to a game was always a good time, but he also didn't want to bombard Ryder over the Bree situation. "Just the three of us?"

Shaking his head, Jackson picked up his own coffee. "No, Bree and Farrow are going, and he invited Tina, too. So, six of us."

Bree, Ryder, and Jackson hanging out together? Levi was sure his skepticism was plain on his face when Jackson only gave him a knowing smile. Plus, even if they'd become friends, Levi wasn't sure how he himself would handle hanging out with Tina and Farrow at the same time. Maybe with all six of them, it wouldn't be too weird, but the potential for awkwardness abounded.

Levi leaned against the counter, met his brother's eyes. "I take it you want to go? You don't think it will be awkward?"

"I do," Jackson confirmed, his smile widening. "It might be a bit awkward at first, but the sooner we all clear the air and get used to it, the better. Plus, baseball game," he added, as though it were obvious.

With a quiet snort of laughter, Levi finally grinned back. Jackson making light of it all was the best sign he could have his brother was truly fine.

And it really was a great day for a baseball game.

"Alright, then. I'm down if you are."

"Good." Jackson picked up the stack of pancakes. "Then let's eat."

⬤⬤⬤⬤⬤

THE DAY WAS BRIGHT, clear, and *hot*. As part of their pre-game ritual, Farrow, Ryder, and Bree sat at the bar of their favorite hole-in-the-wall in Wrigleyville, each with a Chicago handshake —a can of Old Style and a shot of Malört.

The neighborhood had changed quite a bit since the Cubbies' 2016 World Series win; whether or not "new Wrigleyville" was better was up for debate, but some things, thankfully, remained untouched.

One such institution was the Nisei.

A narrow, dimly lit space, the Nisei Lounge boasted of cracked and chipped floor tiles, dark crimson walls and a black ceiling, and rickety stools and tables. Of the things one would expect to find in a bar, there was a patio out back, a questionable photo booth complete with photo wall, a clunky old jukebox, and a single pool table.

Of the things one would not expect, there were too many to name, but Farrow's eyes were often drawn to the singing bass propped up against some board games on a shelf, and the clear glass jar on the far left side of the bar filled with baseballs and a brownish liquid, labeled "Baseball-Infused Malört." It had been there for a good few years; though it could not legally or safely be consumed, it was a nod to the Nisei's tendency to infuse Malört with other things to see how it tasted—such as candy canes for peppermint Malört in December.

And speaking of December (and the unexpected), wrapped around the bright red air duct was a set of garland string lights, and hung from the ceiling with care were Christmas stockings, sparkly snowflakes, paper reindeer, shimmering bits of tinsel, and other Christmas-themed ephemera—including an entire felt advent calendar. More string lights and fluffy red stockings lined the wall opposite the bar.

One of the bartenders had once complained it took her forever to put up the Christmas decorations a few years before, but Farrow suspected that wasn't why they had never been taken down.

It was an atmosphere that unashamedly proclaimed, "Who gives a shit?"

Farrow loved it.

Normally, she would be wearing her Cubs tee, but since they were playing her favorite team, she was wearing her Cardinals tee; so it was that when Levi, Jackson, and Tina walked in and joined them at the bar, the first thing Levi said to her was, "You're a Cardinals fan?"

He didn't sound disgusted, or disappointed, just surprised, so she answered his unasked question with a smile.

"I was born in St. Louis. My parents moved to Chicago when I was three, and since my dad is a Cardinals fan, I grew up one, too. But since Chicago is my home, I'm still a Cubs fan —just not when they're playing the Cardinals."

"I see…"

He didn't sound convinced, and unfortunately Ryder, who'd just finished ordering handshakes for the others, overheard. He called over the two bartenders (thankfully friends of theirs), and they gave her their usual flack, insisting you couldn't be a Cubs fan and a Cardinals fan at the same time, even as they filled the order.

She stuck to her conviction with smiles and laughs, but on the inside the teasing grated a little. She knew they didn't truly disdain her, but neither did she understand why they were so intractable on this subject.

Baseball was baseball, to her mind.

The bar was busy with its pre-game crowd, but thankfully no one was really paying attention; and to Farrow's relief, a couple patrons got the attention of one of the bartenders, pulling them away. Ryder used the opportunity to order another round of Malört for himself, Farrow and Bree; the bartender poured out their shots, and one for himself, and the seven of them held up their glasses in cheers. Farrow went through the ritual, clinking her shot glass against the others, tapping the bottom on the bar top, and knocking it back.

She managed not to grimace—this batch tasted like sour pond water—but reached for her beer for a pull.

Levi used the opening to change the subject, noting Farrow's reaction to the shot with a grin.

He took a seat on the stool next to her. "Not a fan?"

She rolled her eyes. "Is anyone? Ry's the only person I've met who actually likes it."

He shrugged. "It's an acquired taste."

Her eyes narrowed on him. "You like it, too?"

"I do," he laughed. "Why drink it if you don't like it?"

"It's tradition." As if to prove her point, she took a sip of her beer. "I don't always have a shot, but sometimes the occasion calls for it. Besides, I don't think you're actually supposed to like it."

The six of them chatted without any awkwardness for the next half hour, though Levi couldn't help noticing how much happier both Bree and Ryder seemed to be. They were just... brighter, somehow.

But eventually, the game's start time approached, so they headed out to make the few-block walk to the stadium.

The sidewalk was only big enough for two at a time, and almost as if they'd discussed it, Jackson and Tina stepped ahead of everyone else. Bree nodded to Ryder, and went on ahead with Farrow, leaving Levi alone with his friend.

"You probably have questions," Ryder started.

"Yeah."

Ryder stuck his hands in his pockets, blew out a breath. "Look, I've been in love with her forever, and I—"

"Dude, I'm not mad you have feelings for Bree. I just don't get why you never said anything. Instead you let it drag out until Jackson got involved, and you still didn't tell anyone."

"I know." Ry's shoulders slumped a little. "I was an idiot about it. We both were, and I've apologized to Jax. But that's part of why we kept it to ourselves for a little bit. We've both waited so long, now that we've finally made it to this point, we wanted it to be just ours for a bit before we let others in. We wanted to test the waters without all our well-meaning friends hovering around."

Levi thought he understood. He wasn't sure he'd want the eagle eye on him and Farrow either.

"I get it," he said honestly. "And I'm happy for you."

"Thanks, man." Ryder clapped him on the back, and they were silent for a moment. Since he was looking straight ahead, Levi noticed Farrow and Bree glancing back at them; Bree said something to Farrow, then paused while Farrow walked on ahead.

"May I cut in?" she asked, but the question was directed at Ryder.

"Of course," he beamed, then jogged to catch up with Farrow.

Levi raised a brow as Bree fell into step with him.

Wringing her hands, she glanced at him, then away. "You must think I'm a terrible person."

"What?" He stared at her, mouth a little agape. "No, I don't."

"Really?" Her clear green eyes were wide, and a little sad when she blinked at him. "I feel so bad for leading Jackson on. I didn't mean to—but I was a coward. I didn't think Ry would return my feelings, and Jackson is easy to like."

"You don't have to explain, Bree. It's not my business," he assured her. "And Jackson is fine."

"He's the best. And he deserves someone awesome," she smiled sadly. "And I know I don't need to explain, but I wanted to make sure everything is out in the open."

They were across the street from Wrigley Field now, and the group had stopped at the corner, waiting to cross. Perfect time to wrap up this conversation, he thought.

"Well, now it is, and we can all put it behind us."

"Everyone except Ro," Bree chuckled as they turned at the corner with the rest of their group.

"What do you mean?"

Loudly enough for Farrow to hear, Bree said, "I mean, she'll be telling us both 'I told you so' for the rest of our lives."

"Are you kidding?" Farrow turned her head to smirk at her friend. "I'm putting it in my maid of honor speech at your wedding."

Ryder balked a little at the jest, but there was no mistaking the smile he and Bree exchanged.

They breezed through security, and began making their way around what Ro thought of as the 'catacombs' of the stadium— the alternately dimly lit and sunlit wraparound hall filled with concession stands, merch stands, and the restrooms. People moved in every direction, swiveling and sidestepping, zigging and zagging through the crush.

But she'd been held up getting her bag checked by security, and now she was falling behind. She could clearly see the others, only a few feet away, but it had taken her a little longer to pick her way around a line of people. Not to mention her legs were shorter.

Though she knew if she lost them she could easily call or text them, or meet them at their seats, a fissure of panic went through her at the idea they wouldn't notice she'd fallen behind. That they'd forget her, or be too absorbed in each other to notice her absence. Not for the first time, she cursed her social anxiety.

Levi was just in front of her, his tall frame and Bryant jersey right in her line of sight; she thought about calling out, but despite her fears, that smarted her pride, so instead she quickened her pace, turning her body to squeeze between the throng.

She saw the moment Levi's pace slowed a little, when he looked back over his shoulder to check that she was still there. Though he kept moving, when he saw she was still several paces behind, he pivoted slightly to reach his arm back and hold out his hand.

Relief was a warm breeze as she reached out to grasp it, and her heart skittered as he practically pulled her through the crowd, up to his side.

And didn't let go.

It was a simple gesture, but it touched her nonetheless. She smiled at the picture they must have made—the tall, handsome man in his Cubs jersey, and the short, petite woman in her Cardinals tee with "Pujols" emblazoned on the back.

He held on to her hand until they started up the stairs to the next level. The stairwell was less crowded, so it was a logical thing to do, but she was still disappointed by the loss of contact.

When they found their seats, several rows back from the home side dugout, everyone disregarded their assigned seats and coupled up, leaving Farrow sandwiched between Levi and Bree.

Her nervousness faded as the game began, and she settled back in her seat to soak in the familiarity and comfortable camaraderie of a professional baseball game. Though she was rooting for her beloved Cardinals, she wouldn't be terribly upset if her home team won, which helped her relax and enjoy the game even more.

They all got a beer when the vendor came around, which was particularly refreshing in the oppressively sticky humidity; Farrow also savored her ballpark hot dog—a personal tradition —from another vendor, while some of the others eventually got up for other concessions.

She paid special attention to the field whenever the Cardinals were at bat, and was on the edge of her seat every time Pujols came up. Her diligence was eventually rewarded in the fourth inning when he cracked a solo homer into right field, giving the Cardinals a one-nothing lead.

Levi smirked at her triumphant outburst, delighted she was so caught up in the game she didn't realize she'd allowed herself to cheer out loud. When she turned her head to find him smiling at her, he could tell she was surprised, but her own smile didn't dim, and she held his gaze for a beat before returning her attention to the game.

In the sixth inning, Levi noted Ro's change in mood when he felt her tense beside him. He looked away from the field, but didn't see anything unusual around them until he realized what was on the wide screen behind the outfield.

The Kiss Cam.

He felt his own body tense a little—whoever thought subjecting unsuspecting patrons to a public display of affection had obviously never considered that not everyone would want that kind of attention. Most people rolled with it, some even delighted in it, and sometimes it was cute, like when the camera fell on a parent and their child; but other times it was just plain awkward, like when it was obvious the spotlighted pair had no desire to kiss the other.

He'd never considered how he'd handle it, since the odds of the camera landing on him were slim.

But if it landed on him and Farrow…

Perhaps he'd just ask her what she wanted. As much as he wanted to kiss her, he didn't want their first kiss to be forced because of the Kiss Cam, under the watchful eyes of the entire stadium.

Please don't land on us. Please don't land on us.

He froze when, against the odds, the next camera shot cut to their row. He could feel how stricken Farrow was when she braced herself, could see her widened eyes reflected on the giant screen—and felt her relief as his own when they realized the camera was pointing at Bree and Ryder.

Maybe the operators behind the Kiss Cam were more perceptive than it appeared, at least in this instance, as they'd chosen the couple among their group most likely to not mind the attention, and be purposefully enthusiastic in their kiss.

As Levi cheered, he was surprised to see Ro beaming at them, and whooping with the rest of the crowd before the camera moved on.

She did, however, let out an audible sigh of relief once the spotlight was no longer on them. And after that, the game was fairly uneventful; the Cardinals ended up winning four to two, which made Farrow happy.

After the game, they all went back to the Nisei to hang for a bit and wait out the after-game traffic. This time, the bar was packed. They managed to snag a few stools at one end of the bar near the Baseball-Infused Malört jar, Farrow, Bree, and Tina taking a seat while the guys stood behind them.

Levi found he didn't mind not having a seat, as it forced him to stand closer to Farrow than he normally would. He stood more to her side, and instead of leaning against the back of the chair, she leaned a little into him. If he questioned whether she was doing it on purpose, all doubt vanished when she turned her head to give him a sultry smile.

Eventually, Tina stretched and indicated her desire to go home.

"Did you guys drive in?" Bree asked.

"No, we hopped on the Swift," Jackson told her, referring to the L's yellow line, which ran from Skokie into the city.

"Perfect," she beamed. "Then we can all walk back to Addison together."

As they headed back in the direction of the field toward the L stop, they once again paired off, with Jackson and Tina up front, Ryder and Bree in the middle, and Levi and Farrow bringing up the rear.

"Do you have any other plans for the day?" he asked her.

She shrugged. "Probably just order take out and read a book. You?"

"Probably play video games with Jackson."

He caught the little quirk at the side of her mouth.

"What?"

She shook her head, her smile widening. "Nothing. Just, for some reason I pictured you being super competitive at video games."

"Oh, he is," Ryder called back over his shoulder. "Dude is merciless, especially in Mario Party."

Levi only smirked. "You're welcome to join us."

"Nah." Ryder slung his arm over Bree's shoulders. "Bree and I are going out to dinner."

As they approached the station, Levi realized he wasn't ready to part ways with Farrow yet. But she, Ryder, and Bree would get on a red line train going in a different direction than the rest of them. As if thinking the same thing, Bree looked back at Farrow.

"You gonna be alright?" she asked.

"Yeah," Farrow assured her. "My place isn't too far from my stop."

"Shit." Ryder dropped his arm and turned so he was walking sideways. "I'm sorry, Ro, I didn't think."

"I'll be fine, Ry."

"Did I miss something?" Levi asked.

"They're just worried about me being alone," Farrow informed him. "But it's nothing I haven't done before."

"Ah." Levi flicked a glance at Ryder, caught his subtle nod. "What if I walk you home?"

Farrow tilted her head. "Isn't that out of your way?"

"So? Jax and Tina can wait for me once they get back to the Skokie station."

She considered him a moment, and he spent that moment worrying she'd say no; she likely would be fine, but he wanted to prolong his time with her.

And dare he hope she returned the sentiment.

"Okay." Her smile was slow and warm. "Thank you."

He saw the knowing look Bree and Ryder exchanged; perhaps he was being a little obvious, but they also knew Farrow best, so perhaps he should take it as a vote of confidence.

As they entered the station, Levi explained the situation to Jackson and Tina, who smirked and assured him they would wait—if he needed them to. Ignoring her, Levi followed Farrow and the others to wait for a train going toward the city center.

They didn't have to wait long, thankfully, and the ride was as uneventful and full of awkward eye-contact avoidance as usual.

When they reached the stop closest to Bree's apartment, she and Ryder said their farewells and got off, leaving their friends to be alone at last.

"You think he'll finally make a move?" Ryder wondered aloud.

Bree smiled, slid her hand into his. "If he doesn't, I think she'll ask him to stay."

After a few more minutes on the train, Farrow and Levi reached Farrow's stop at Fullerton. They exited the station in silence, Levi following just beside her as he considered what to say. Perhaps he should take Ryder's example and ask if Farrow wanted to grab dinner with him.

It was a nice neighborhood—an area of Lincoln Park close to the zoo—and he'd spotted several interesting-looking restaurants. He was still debating when they made a turn, and Farrow indicated it was her street.

As they approached her gate, she pulled out her keys, clutching them like a lifeline. She was clearly nervous, but he couldn't tell if he made her nervous, or if she was making herself nervous by overthinking. Just in case, he made sure to put a little bit of space between them when they stopped at her gate, and slid his hands into his pockets.

She unlocked it, pushed it open a few inches, the high-pitched groan of the iron piercing the silence, lingering like a question between them. She paused to turn back toward him, and he wondered what she was thinking when she tilted her head up at him, assessing as her fingers fiddled with a keychain of a wooden bat on her keyring.

"Thanks for walking me home," she said softly.

"You're welcome, anytime."

Should he kiss her? Hug her? Wave goodbye? All of the above?

Shit, why was this so hard?

When she said nothing further, he concluded a simple farewell might be best, and gave her a friendly smile.

"I'll see you at practice on Monday."

She nodded. "Yeah. See you then."

He nodded back before turning around and heading down the sidewalk. *Well that wasn't awkward at all,* he thought, the shrill creaking of the gate opening wider reverberating around in his head.

And then, the unmistakable sound of her voice calling his name.

His feet halted, and his body turned halfway around before his brain fully registered she'd called after him. She stood, one hand on a rung of the open gate, teeth pulling at her bottom lip as he waited for her to speak.

Finally she said, "Do you…want to come in?"

Hell yes.

"Sure."

Her smile was so shy and relieved, his heart deflated and re-inflated all at once. He was by her side in seconds—he hadn't gotten very far down the street—and before he knew it he was on the other side of the gate as she closed and locked it. He shot off a quick text to Jackson (who wouldn't tease him) not to wait for him, then followed her quietly into the building and up into her apartment.

SIX

FARROW DID her best to remember to breathe as she switched on lights in her apartment. She'd wavered and waffled, but she'd done it. She'd invited Levi inside, and he'd accepted.

Now what?

Well, she knew what she wanted to do with him, but she wasn't sure she'd have the guts to initiate anything. Perhaps asking him in was as far as her boldness went. She didn't do this kind of thing. Not really. It'd been so long since she was genuinely interested in someone she wasn't quite sure how to be natural in this situation.

And they'd been circling each other for weeks now; the idea that it had all been leading here set her already fraying nerves on edge.

She focused on stowing her things, and when she'd hung her keys and bag on their proper hooks by the door, she turned to find him simply taking in her space. His eyes roamed over the unit's faux fireplace with built in shelving, lingering on the shelves stuffed to the max with books before flicking around the rest of the open living and dining area.

She assumed he liked what he saw, as there was a wistful sort of smile curving on one side of his mouth.

There was an exposed brick wall on one side of the apartment, so she'd gone with a mostly industrial aesthetic, with a bit of mid-century modern and boho pieces thrown in. Her large dark wood dining set sat in the front room, flanked on three sides by tall windows, and surrounded by a jungle of plants. Between the dining area and the living room was the foyer with the fireplace and shelves; she'd stuck an electric wood burning stove-style heater in the fireplace space, and placed two cozy, olive green wingback chairs on either side.

Separating the foyer from the living room was a wall with a wide archway, where she'd strung colorful beaded curtains and tied them back. A long, leather sectional in an orange-brown color spanned part of the living room, buttery soft and inviting with the plush pillows in cream and olive green she'd decorated it with. A large, industrial trunk acted as her coffee table, while a rug with varying shades of green, blue, and orange added a pop of color, as did the green floor cushions peeking out from under the sofa. She had a decently sized TV atop a decorative wooden sideboard, and her record player and collection had their own setup on the far side of the room.

Wherever there was wall space, she'd hung an eclectic collection of paintings, prints, and wall art, while some family photos sat on her side tables and the mantle, along with some candles and decorative pieces.

When his gaze finally landed back on her, he was grinning from ear to ear.

"This is a really nice space," he said.

"Thank you. I can't take full credit for that, though; Bree helped a lot." Some of her nerves flittered away. "I bet I can guess what your favorite part is."

"I bet you can, too."

"I spent a lot of time organizing those bookshelves." She stared fondly at all her precious books as she walked toward them, taking a moment to run her fingers over some of the spines.

"That's not it," he said quietly. "That's a nice bonus, but that's not my favorite part."

Brows drawn together, she looked back at him, met his steady gaze. "It's not? Then what is?"

"You." His eyes never left her face, and her heart felt like it'd been knocked out of the park. "This is your space, and I'm in it with you."

"Oh," was all she could manage to say through the tightening in her throat. After a beat of silence, she cleared it, but her voice sounded a little shaky when she said, "Well, I invited you."

"Yes, you did." He took a few steps closer to her. "Why?"

"Why?"

"What do you want to do now that I'm here?" He clarified.

Oh, so many things, she thought, her gaze automatically tracking down and up his body, lingering on his mouth. He took another step closer, and her face must have given her thoughts away because then he took another. He didn't stop until he was only a few inches from her, and he reached out to tug gently on her ponytail until she was looking up at him and—

Holy curveballs, what even are words?

"Tell me what you want, Farrow," he murmured, his breath, hot on her ear, causing her to shiver.

Since she'd lost the connection to her brain that understood what words were, she answered him by rising on her toes, grasping his face in her hands, and yanking his mouth to hers. His response was immediate, the hand in her hair pulling at her hair tie until her waves spilled down her back and over her shoulders, while his other arm clamped around her waist and pressed her up against him. His fingers curled in her hair when she hummed against his lips.

Need had her hands running over his chest when his tongue

darted into her mouth, hot and seeking. She felt a bit desperate as her fingers trailed lower, began lifting the hem of his shirt higher. She felt his small huff of laughter at her insistence; then he lifted his arms so she could pull the jersey over his head.

She tossed his shirt toward one of the chairs, but had no time to to make sure it actually landed. But she found she didn't care, as Levi's hands tugging up her own shirt was the reason for her distraction.

When he had her top off, he, unlike her, simply tossed it aside. But she didn't have time to see where it landed either, as he'd then bent to grip her waist and lift her; her legs automatically wrapped around him as she took advantage of her newfound height to nip up his neck to his earlobe.

He groaned as he turned in the direction of the living room, letting out a somewhat breathless, "Bed?"

She shocked herself by saying, "Couch is fine," and switching her attention to his other earlobe. But he took her at her word, maneuvering over to the sectional and dropping down onto it so that he sat, and she was straddling his lap.

Then his lips were on hers again, his fingers slipping the straps of her bra down her shoulders before tugging her bra down nearly to her waist. She was about to point out he could simply remove the garment, when he took a breast in his mouth, cupping the other in one hand, and rational thought strayed like a wild pitch.

There was only Levi—his hands and lips on her, her body against his, his smooth skin and muscles under her hands. She wriggled against him, the movement instinctive and pleading. He grinned as he bit lightly at her nipple before soothing it with his tongue and turning his attention to the other.

She didn't realize she'd begun to rock against him until his hands gripped her bottom, steadying her movements.

She wanted to protest, but one of his deft hands quickly tugged open the button and zipper on her shorts before maneuvering inside, down, over.

The gasp this elicited from her was one of pleasurable torture, as his finger rubbing her just there only increased the ache.

"That's it, baby," he purred, and she gloried in the heat spreading through her body. Her own hands wandered down, reaching around him to undo his shorts. He lifted his hips a few inches so she could slide them down along with his boxers, freeing him to her greedy hands. He hissed out an oath of pleasure when she wrapped a hand around him, pumped slowly.

This proved too distracting, and his hands came back to her face, pulled her in for a kiss. "Condom," he rasped, his voice thick with desire.

"I have a box in my nightstand." Farrow tilted her head, deliberately ran her thumb over the tip of him.

His head fell to the back of the couch on an intake of breath, and he reached up to cup her breasts as his eyes met hers. A slow, wide grin broke out over her face, and she leaned forward to rub her lips over his before nuzzling his neck.

"I may have bought it this morning."

"A whole box?" He sputtered out a laugh, causing his body to jerk slightly; she let go of him, rose to slide off him.

"We don't have to use them all tonight." Smirking, she dashed into her room, located the box of condoms and drew out a foil packet. As she hurried back to the living room, she imagined she must look ridiculous, still half dressed with her bra practically around her waist, but with the way Levi was looking at her she found she didn't care.

He reached for her as she approached, and she settled easily back into his lap. She raised a brow as she opened the packet. "Want me to do the honors?"

Just the suggestion made him twitch against her, so she took that as a yes, rolled it teasingly down his length. Then she came up on her knees to pull off her shorts, but he wrapped his arms around her and flipped them so her back was on the couch; she lifted her hips when he hooked his fingers in her waistband, but he only pulled her shorts and underwear down to her calves, began kissing his way up her body.

"In a hurry?" Her laugh was cut off by a moan when his finger circled her center once again.

"You could say that," he said before pressing his lips to hers, slow and deep.

She hummed in pleasure, her hands stroking down his back before gripping him, guiding him to her entrance. And when he slid into her, she was lost.

They moved together, taking cues from sighs and moans as words were once again beyond comprehension. She reveled in the smoothness of his skin, the warmth and pressure of his body against hers. She wanted to wrap her legs around him, but was restricted by her shorts—yet there was something arousing about not being fully undressed.

So instead she squeezed her legs tighter, gasping as a bolt of pleasure shot through her, the ignition of the crest she longed for. In response, he slowed his movements, rocking into her in a way that ensured she could feel all of him. She blinked, gasping, arching as the sweet, tingling sensation swept through her, slowly, like a molten starburst—as did the lovely ache in her heart that told her just how connected to him she felt.

She let it ride, clinging to him and running her lips over his shoulder, his neck, his jaw as sensation eased and his pace picked up again. It wasn't long before he sucked in a breath, clamped his mouth over hers as his movement stilled, slowed again.

She could feel his heartbeat hammering against her, seemingly mingling with her own. Tracing his cheek lightly with the tips of her fingers when he pressed a softer kiss to her lips, she sighed in satisfaction and contentment. He leaned his forehead against hers, and she opened her eyes to find his staring longingly at her face.

She bit her lip. "What?"

He smiled, brushing some of her hair from her face. "I just like looking at you."

"Sometimes I think my heart will stop just looking at you."

His brows shot up, and her eyes widened when she realized what she'd said. *Obsessive, much?* she thought. She made to sit up, but didn't get far, as she was still pinned under him—and he was still inside her.

Realizing this, he trailed a hand down her body until it rested on her hip, all the while keeping his eyes on her face. "I think you made my heart stop just now," he told her.

She'd been staring at his hand on her hip, but now blinked back up at him. He grinned before giving her one more languid kiss and pulling out of her.

"Better clean up," he pointed out.

He carefully pushed up and off the couch, kicking off the rest of his clothes before going to the bathroom. She couldn't help the idiotic grin that overcame her as he waltzed naked across her apartment.

She tugged her bra back into place and pulled up her underwear, but her shorts joined his on the floor before she went to her ensuite to clean up. He was sitting on the couch in his boxers when she returned, and raised a brow when he saw she was half-clothed.

Turning on the charm, he said, "What'd you get dressed for?"

She sent him a sultry smile as she returned to the couch; once again, he automatically held out his arms for her, wrapping them around her as she slid down and curled into him.

"What did *you* get dressed for?" she posed back.

"I didn't want to leave a butt print on this couch," he admitted with a half-laugh.

She chuckled. "We probably left lots of prints on this couch."

He tipped his head. "Fair point."

Considering how long he might want to stay, she pulled back a little to face him. "Are you hungry?"

"I could eat."

"How about I order a pizza?"

His brows shot up as a grin suffused his face. "Sex *and* pizza? Be still my beating heart."

"I'll take that as a yes to pizza." She grinned back, picked up her phone. "And the sex and pizza's not just for you, you know."

"Oh, I know." He slid his arm back around her middle. "And I intend to make it worth your while."

They ordered takeout as she'd originally planned, indulging in cupped pepperoni pizza with drizzles of hot honey on top, washed down with red wine. The difference was there was definitely no reading—that, and they ate at the coffee table, lazing about on the couch in their underwear, sharing their favorite YouTube shows and videos with each other.

Why hadn't she done anything like this before?

She'd eaten from her couch and coffee table before, sure, but there was no rule that said she had to be fully clothed in her own home. Maybe it was too soon to think it, but she hoped she'd have many more nights like this with Levi, relaxed and happy.

When there were only a few slices of pizza left, Levi leaned back with a groan.

"Why do I always eat too much pizza?"

Farrow shrugged. "Because it's pizza?"

"That could be it." He blew out a breath, draping an arm over his stomach. They sat in silence for a few moments, using the lull in conversation to contemplate what came next. For his part, Levi wondered how to introduce a weightier subject, one he wasn't sure he had a right to ask about until now.

But if he and Farrow were starting something, he needed to understand why she was hurting, and she needed to trust him. Watching her carefully, he sat up a little.

"Have you enjoyed playing on the team?" he asked.

Her eyes whipped to his, a question in the lift of her brow when she answered. "I've loved it. I thought that was obvious."

"It is. But you were hesitant at first," he reminded her. "The Longhorns are all the better for having you on the team, so I want to make sure you're happy."

"Well, I am, thank you," she said, patting his knee.

"I think we've got a shot at winning the championship," he said evenly.

"So do I." She cocked her head. "If you think we can win, why do you sound so...cautious?"

"Because if they also keep winning games, we'll be playing the Redcoats again."

Farrow straightened slowly as understanding dawned. Concerned at the blank expression that had morphed her into a statue, he pressed on.

"I can't keep ignoring the effect a particular player had on you, and Ry and Andrew," he said softly. "Who exactly is Greg Wyatt, and what did he do to piss you guys off so much?"

Farrow took a long, slow breath. She was quiet for so long he began to think she wasn't going to answer, but finally, she took another breath and looked back at him.

"Greg was an old family friend," she started, wringing her hands. "Or at least, our fathers were friends. So when Greg's dad died, my parents did their best to help his mom out, including financial aid. He got a baseball scholarship to college, but they helped her cover the rest of the expenses. He went to the same college as me."

She paused, and he waited for her to gather her thoughts as she reached for her wine, took a steadying sip. Her expression was distant when she continued, "I started seeing another side of him there. It was little things at first, and I thought maybe he was just grieving, lashing out. But by the time senior year rolled around, he gambled a lot, and I wondered where he was getting the money to do so, especially since he seemed to lose most of the time.

"Long story short, I discovered he was throwing games to win bets. I told my parents and reported him, and when the school looked into it, they found out he'd thrown some games in order to pay some of his gambling debt."

When she went quiet for another stretch, Levi prompted, "I'm guessing he lost his scholarship."

She nodded. "He was expelled. And in retaliation...he went to visit my sister. She's only a few years younger than me, but she was just a freshman at the time. Only nineteen. Bree and I were on the softball team, and our team had made it to the state championship; a couple hours before the game, I got a cryptic text from Greg. A picture of my sister with a beer in her hand, looking out of it."

She rubbed her palm over her chest as though it ached, and her other hand had clenched into a fist around the stem of her glass. When her free hand came down to rest on her knee, Levi laid a hand over hers, rubbed his thumb over the back of her hand. "That must have been scary."

"Very." She paused again, turned her hand over to lace her fingers through his. "I immediately contacted my parents, and his mom. He wouldn't take his mom's calls, but my sister eventually responded to my messages asking where she was. By the time we got to her, she was very drunk, and he was nowhere to be found. She assured us he was coming back, and was heartbroken when he didn't.

"Needless to say, I didn't make it to the game. We lost. It was supposed to be the last game of my senior year. Instead, I missed it, and hadn't played a game until you asked me to join the Longhorns."

His eyes widened. "Wait, you hadn't played in...what, three years?"

She shook her head. "Just about. I still played catch with Ry, or Bree, and went to a batting cage. But never played in a game. Couldn't face it, I guess."

All he could think to say was, "I'm sorry. I'm sorry he did that to your sister."

"It's my fault," she said absently. "He did it to get back at me. And his revenge was twofold, since my team lost because of me."

"Whoa, hold on." Levi straightened, gripped her shoulders so he could turn her to face him. "It is *not* your fault. You didn't make that bastard do anything, he did it all on his own. And as for the rest—you win as a team, you lose as a team. Don't put that on yourself."

"We might have won if I'd been there," she pointed out, chin raising just a little.

"Might have, sure, but you don't know that you would have," he said firmly. "You're not giving your team enough credit if you think you alone could've made a difference. And would you feel any better about missing the game if they had won?"

"I...I suppose I wouldn't." She let out a quiet, humorless scoff, set her wine glass down on the coffee table. "All this time I thought...you're right. I haven't been giving my team credit. They were a really good team, with or without me."

"We all feel a little guilt arrogance from time to time," he assured her.

Her brow arched. "Guilt arrogance?"

"Yeah, you know—when you take the blame for something not your fault. Like survivor's guilt, but without the death. I think we do it because pretending we could have changed things means we still have some semblance of control, even though in reality we have none. You felt bad you couldn't prevent what happened to your sister, so you convinced yourself it was your fault. And you hated missing out on the championship game, so you told yourself you would have won if you'd been there."

She inclined her head. "I know all too well going over what ifs can't change the past."

"If you can accept it's not your fault, do you think you can handle it if we play against the Redcoats in the championship?"

She considered a moment, weighing everything Levi had said. She hadn't come this close to closure over the Wyatt situation before, but she could feel something new taking root in those buried feelings. It might take a little bit longer for full acceptance to grow, but for the first time, she thought she could get there.

"Yes," she finally nodded. "I can handle it. And I believe we'll win—as a team."

He smiled. "Good."

"Thank you, Levi." She leaned in, gave him a soft kiss. When he hummed, slid a hand over her bare back, she remembered they were still in only their underwear. Grinning, she gave his bottom lip a light tug with her teeth. "Why don't we move to the bedroom, and I can thank you properly."

Shaking his head, he slid his other arm under her legs, pulled her into his lap, and lifted her as he stood.

"I told you," he grinned as he carried her to the bedroom, "I'm going to make it worth your while."

They took their time, no longer in such a rush to get their hands on each other—and he made good on his promise, going over every inch of her he'd missed the first time. Afterward, they showered together, making plans for the next weekend in between bouts of teasing each other.

It felt so normal, and just…right. Levi had a feeling he and Farrow would have some of their most interesting conversations in the shower.

And it felt just as right when he stayed. When, after he'd settled in beside her, he looked over at her, already resting comfortably against her pillow.

"Today was a damn good day," he said.

Though she yawned through her smile, her eyes were bright. "It really was."

It really was. And, he thought as his eyes closed, he could get used to this.

SEVEN

"WHAT DO you mean Billy quit the team?"

The other cleat had to drop sometime, didn't it? Farrow thought as Ryder began to pace. She'd had an excellent night—and morning—with Levi over the weekend, and now they'd arrived at practice only to learn some very inconvenient news.

Facing the team gathered in the dugout, Andrew took off his hat, ran a hand over his hair before setting the hat back on his head.

"I had to have a hard talk with him yesterday about his recent behavior," he explained, gesturing for a fuming Ryder to sit. "I told him as long as he continued to have a bad attitude and be rude to his teammates, then I'd have to bench him. He opted to be benched permanently."

"Good riddance," Levi muttered.

"I'm not disagreeing," said Ryder, "but now we're down a player—again. And the playoffs start next week."

Ever the optimist, Jackson pointed out, "We still have enough players to fill the field, plus one more."

Eddie shifted nervously. "Yeah, but only ten players is cutting it pretty close."

Farrow pursed her lips as a thought occurred to her, but she decided to let it stew a moment first while she listened to the discussion.

"What about your brother Tom?" Andrew asked Manny. "Does he still play?"

"He might," Manny said skeptically. "But I wouldn't count on him giving up his current party boy lifestyle."

Andrew turned to Henry. "Cat's brother?"

Henry shook his head. "James is on a work trip in England for the summer."

"I could ask my friend Robbie Martin," Knight offered. "We were on our high school team together, but he's only played pick up games since."

Andrew shook his head. "Then he doesn't qualify. Players had to have played at at least collegiate level to join this league."

"Then that rules out my friend Benwick, too," Fred considered. "Do any of us know anyone else?"

The more Farrow thought about it, the better her idea seemed. With the silence that followed Fred's question, she straightened, grinned at Ryder. "I think I know the perfect person."

"Who?" Ryder frowned, then his eyes widened as it hit him. "No. Wait. Do you think...?"

"Who are you talking about?" Brandon asked.

"Someone we all know," Farrow shared with a secret smile. "And she's already got her own jersey. Bree."

Fred folded his arms. "The cheerleader plays baseball?"

"We played collegiate softball together," Farrow explained, arched a brow. "Where do you think she learned those cheers?"

"How good is she?"

"Does it matter? We don't have very many options," Henry put in, then graced them all with his teasing smile. "Besides, if Farrow and Ryder are vouching for her, then she's definitely better than Billy."

The joke got a few laughs of agreement, and succeeded in loosening them all up a bit.

Levi's smirk turned wicked. "Wouldn't it just stick in Billy's craw that we replaced him with another woman?"

"And the kicker?" Farrow mirrored Levi's expression with her own smirk. "Second base is her main position."

"Alright." Andrew held up a hand for attention. "If we all agree, we'll ask Bree if she wants to play. If she agrees, we'll have her try out at our next practice. All in favor?"

Some hands went up slower than others, but not by much; within a few seconds, it was decided.

"Okay." Andrew nodded. "Ro, Ry, I'll leave it to you to reach out to her. Everyone else keep thinking in case she says no."

⁑⁑⁑

SHE DIDN'T SAY NO.

Farrow was only surprised her reaction was less enthusiastic than expected. When she and Ryder had explained Billy's departure, Bree had been properly horrified. But when they'd asked her if she'd be willing to replace him, she'd turned to them with her face set in an uncharacteristically stern expression.

"Of course I'll play," she assured them. "When's the next practice?"

"Tomorrow," Ry told her.

Bree's face lit with a bubbly smile, and she even did a little bounce on her toes. "Great. Just let me dust off my gear."

There it is, thought Farrow.

When the three of them showed up at practice the next day, Bree was all warm smiles and energy. If any of their teammates had doubts about her switching from softball, they were erased when practice began in earnest.

Bree might have been a sweet, cheerful sort, but on the field she was a beast. Even better was her base running—Bree was a

103

speed demon, which would give them an advantage in stealing bases. Even Farrow had never managed to throw her out at two.

Though she easily adjusted to the different base lead off rules, it did take Bree some time to get used to hitting baseballs instead of softballs. But when she could hit some of Ryder's full-speed pitches, he assured her she'd be able to hit off other pitchers.

His theory was proven correct in their next game when Bree slammed the ball into right field during her first at bat, and turned what would have been a single into a double just through her running. They won that game three to nothing, and carried that momentum with them through their remaining games.

When, in the deciding game, Brandon cracked a double in the last inning with two outs still to go, the whole team—and their fan section in the bleachers, which, thanks to Tina, had grown to include Nora Dashwood—leapt to their feet. The hit brought Knight safely across home plate, and gave the Longhorns a one-run lead.

Even without any more runs, it was official—they were going to the championship.

And, it was discovered a few days later, so were the Redcoats. It wasn't surprising news, but it seemed they'd blasted through their opponents on their way to get to the top, if the reports of their victory were accurate. They'd been merciless last time they played the Longhorns; Levi expected this time would be even more intense.

As he lay in Farrow's bed the night before the game, her warm body snug against his, her head nestled under his chin, he couldn't help but be a little worried. While he didn't doubt the Longhorns could win, he was sure the Redcoats would have something up their sleeve.

"You know, I'm starting to find your thinking face endearing," Farrow murmured against his chest.

He lifted his head slightly to look at her, but all he could see was the top of her head.

"You can't even see my face."

"I can feel you thinking too hard." Her fingers began to graze lazily across his chest. "I assume it's about the game tomorrow?"

He blew out a breath. "Yeah. I guess I'm just anxious."

"Me too." She shifted so that her arms were crossed against his chest and she could look into his eyes. "But we can handle whatever they throw at us. I believe that."

"I believe it, too." He stroked a hand down her back.

"Good." She leaned forward, pressed her lips to his. "Then we'd better get some sleep."

Before she could roll away, his arms tightened around her.

"I'm having a little trouble shutting my brain off. It might take me a while to fall asleep."

"Hmm." Her lips quirked, and she slid a leg over until she lay astride him. "Perhaps I can help you with that."

⟨⟨⟨⟨⟩⟩⟩⟩

SUNNY SKIES, warm weather with a light breeze, and freshly mowed grass greeted Levi and Farrow when they arrived at the field.

It was a perfect day for baseball, a feeling that lifted the somewhat somber mood of the team, even if only a little.

It was lifted a little more when their friends and family started arriving in the bleachers. Tina and Cat sat together, as usual, and were joined now by Nora, who'd been happy to reconnect with her old friends. Frank and his wife came to cheer them on, as they had on and off through the season—there was no way Frank was missing the championship game, though.

Even Levi and Jackson's brothers had all come—but thankfully kept their mother from attending. Levi had yet to meet

105

Farrow's parents or sister, but he knew she'd told them they shouldn't come, and why. But she'd promised to let them know the outcome of the game as soon as it was over.

Despite the support, it seemed everyone was a little apprehensive about playing the Redcoats.

They warmed up as usual, but it was quiet, especially in comparison to the other team shouting and laughing during their own warm up. More than ever, Levi couldn't shake the feeling he was missing something.

And finally, when both teams were huddled in their dugouts awaiting the start of the game, he realized what it was when he ran a watchful eye over the other team.

He blinked, did a double take. He couldn't believe what he was seeing. "Is that...is that Billy?"

The others looked toward the Redcoats' dugout with various expressions of horror and confusion. Sure enough, Billy's ruddy face was among the bright red ball caps, and he leaned against the chainlink fence as if he didn't have a care in the world.

Bree pursed her lips. "Well, that's bad news bears."

"Son of bitch," Ryder growled, then turned away, resisting the urge to punch something. Bree laid a hand on his arm.

"That weasel." Farrow narrowed her eyes. "He's probably told them about all our plays and signals."

"Then we'll just have to think of new ones," Ryder said firmly.

"Let's not worry about that yet," Jackson suggested. "He might not have said anything."

Levi shook his head. "Sorry, Jax, but the chances of that are slim. He would see it as the perfect revenge."

"That's just great," Fred grumbled.

"So we test it out." Knight stood as he spoke, his deep voice and height giving him a commanding presence. "Start thinking of new signs, and if we notice during the first inning we're getting stonewalled, we scrap the old ones."

"A sound strategy," Andrew agreed, then flicked a calculating eye at Farrow and Bree. "Ro, Bree, do you guys remember any of the signs your softball team used?"

Bree gave him a grin edged with razors. "You bet we do."

"Alright," Andrew nodded. "We'll keep that in reserve. Now let's get ready to bat. Henry leads us off. Bree, I hope you don't mind, but Manny will be your designated hitter. You'll still run as an alternate."

Bree held up her hands. "Fine by me."

Henry and the next two on deck grabbed up their bats and helmets, started taking practice swings while the other team filtered onto the field. Andrew went to stand by third base.

From his stance at second, Billy sneered at his former team, but Farrow barely spared him a glance. She took stock of the rest of the Redcoats' team as they began to warm up. She was surprised to see Elton in right field instead of her nemesis. With a sinking feeling, her gaze swept over the diamond to home plate, where her eyes met the smug face of Greg Wyatt.

He winked at her before pulling his catcher's mask over his confident smirk.

Enjoy it while it lasts, she thought, narrowing her eyes. *You haven't won yet.*

The bastard.

As if sensing her stewing in her heightened emotions, Levi came up beside her, curled his fingers through the holes of the fence. "You ready?"

"As I'll ever be."

He only quirked a brow.

"He can't disconcert me now," Farrow said definitively. "This time I know what to expect, and I'm more determined than ever to take him down."

"Then let's kick some Redcoats ass," he said, pushing off the fence.

Henry played it smart at bat, waiting out a few pitches

before taking a swing. The ball sailed into left center field, earning him a single.

Farrow watched Wyatt and Billy carefully when Jackson stepped up to the box. After testing out a couple pitches, Andrew called to him and went through a round of signals, including the one for "steal."

When Henry took his lead off as usual, she thought she saw Billy give some kind of signal to Wyatt, who in turn gave one to their pitcher, Denny—though she couldn't be sure it wasn't a normal exchange between pitcher and catcher.

But she was sure of it when Denny hitched his leg and made to throw. Henry went for it, sprinting toward second; but instead of throwing the pitch, Denny pivoted and threw the ball to Crawford, their shortstop, already waiting at the bag.

Henry basically slid right into Crawford's tag. Billy's cackle as Henry was declared out was unmistakable. Jackson swung at the next pitch, hitting a grounder to third, where Willoughby scooped it up easily and threw for the out at one.

Ryder was next to bat. He'd noticed Billy's indication to Wyatt just before Henry tried to steal second, and wondered how he could best rub it in their smug faces. Deciding to test the theory a bit more, he watched a couple pitches go by before stepping a foot out of the box and turning to Andrew. He gave their sign for "bunt," to which Andrew looked momentarily confused; but he must have understood Ryder's game, because he nodded and gave the same sign back.

A surreptitious glance at Billy showed him signaling Wyatt.

Biting back a smirk, Ryder stepped back into the box. As Denny took his stance, Ryder crouched to bunt, noticed the fielders take some steps inward. But just as Denny reared back and threw, Ryder straightened into his normal stance and swung at the next pitch—hard. He took off for first as the fly careened into center field, but didn't make it to the bag before he saw the beefy arm of Forster reach up to catch it.

Damn it. Can of corn.

He jogged back to the dugout with a huff, dragged off his helmet with a rough shake of his head. "They definitely know our signs," he hissed, tucking the helmet under his arm.

"Billy's even cuing them," Farrow added. Already strapped into her shin guards, she pulled the chest protector over her head.

"Alright," Andrew nodded firmly. "You and Bree will teach us the new signs before the next inning. For now, take the field as though nothing is amiss."

Ryder pounded his fist into his glove. "They won't know what hit 'em."

Smiling mischievously, Bree held up her phone as the grinding tones of Hendrix's "Wild Thing" eked out through the small speaker. Ry rolled his eyes, but smiled as he turned out of the dugout.

It certainly served to relax the team, and they filtered onto the field, tossing some balls around as Ryder threw a few warm up pitches. The between-inning routine was disrupted when there was a bit of a commotion from the Redcoats' dugout.

Billy stormed out, pointed an accusing finger at Bree. "What is *she* doing here?"

Evidently, he hadn't noticed her before, but in her position at second, the strawberry blonde ponytail pulled through her cap glinting a bit coppery in the sunshine, she stood out among the rest of her team.

It was Levi who came to her defense, folding his arms as he stared Billy down. "Replacing you. Seeing as you defected and all."

"Is there a problem here?" The ump demanded. Andrew wasn't far behind.

"They have a new player on their team." Billy pointed at Bree again.

"Indeed we do," Andrew said dryly. "Did you think we wouldn't find someone to replace you when you quit?"

"Rather hypocritical of you to be upset, isn't it?" Knight

asked, his position at third giving him a front row seat to the spectacle. "You're a new player for the Redcoats yourself, so what's it to you that we have one?"

"She's a girl!" Billy protested.

Bree's chin came up, but she affected confusion. "I am? Why didn't anyone tell me before?"

While her team chuckled, Billy insisted, "She can't play. I've been part of this league all season—she hasn't."

"She has all the right qualifications, and board approval," Andrew informed him, his face stony.

The ump nodded. "As I'm aware. There's no cause for all this fuss."

"Now that that's settled," Ryder said from the mound, "Shall we get on with the game?"

Everyone agreed as a reluctant Billy shuffled back to the dugout, and after that the inning was anticlimactic; Ryder struck out the first three batters—Thorpe, Elliot, and Denny—in a row. Whether it was Billy's attack on Bree that fueled the Torch's fire, Levi couldn't say, but he was certainly living up to his moniker today.

As soon as the last out was called, those on field jogged back for a team huddle, gathering around Bree and Farrow so as to block the other team's view of them.

"Our coach liked to disguise the real sign in between a bunch of other signs," Bree explained. "When she tapped her nose, that was the indication the next sign was the real one."

They decided which signs were most important at the moment, and she and Farrow quickly demonstrated the motions for swing away, hold, and steal.

"That ought to throw them off," Henry grinned cheekily.

Unfortunately, though they did succeed in confusing Billy's efforts to reveal their signs, they didn't manage any runs that inning. Levi led off by hitting a fly into left field, which was caught by Thorpe. Brandon was more successful, hitting a grounder too far up the middle for Billy or Crawford to reach and making it safely to first. They were optimistic when Knight smacked the ball deep into right center, but Forster was faster than he looked and managed to snag it. Though Brandon tagged up and made it to second, he was picked off by Denny and Crawford during Manny's at-bat, which meant Manny would be leading them off next inning.

Thankfully their luck on the field held. Just as had been the case with them, the Redcoats' power hitters were next in the lineup.

A overly-confident Willoughby swung at the first pitch; though he managed to connect, and hard, the grounder was easily swept up by Bree and thrown to Henry at first. Crawford managed a single into left field, and everyone on the field became hyper-aware as Forster made his way to the plate. He too, swung at the first pitch, and hit a liner right at Ryder, who stumbled back a little even as the ball smacked into his glove just under his chin.

Sanderson was next at bat; either he had more patience than his teammates, or he'd been given a signal to wait. Instinct had Farrow tracking Crawford's movements.

Was it her, or was he taking a little bit of a longer lead than before? She braced herself, shifting her feet just a little to be ready for a throw, giving her own signal to Ryder. He nodded, wound up.

Just as he released the ball, Crawford took off. Farrow straightened as she caught the ball, already turning. Her throw reached Levi's glove seconds before Crawford, who hadn't even attempted to slide, and he was easily tagged. Considering his roll in tagging out Brandon, Ro considered it poetic justice.

She didn't miss the way Crawford threw his helmet on the ground when he made it back to the dugout. As she was on deck, she determined to be on alert if she got on base.

When Manny returned to the batter's box, he ripped one into left field, earning him a single. Andrew called time to switch in Bree as the runner as Farrow stepped up to the plate.

"We meet again," Wyatt said silkily.

Farrow ignored him, glancing at Andrew, who was giving her the signal to swing away. With a runner like Bree on base, her goal was to advance her friend as much as possible. With that in mind, she stepped around the plate to bat lefty instead, making it easier for her to aim to hit the ball into right field.

On her first attempt, she fouled the ball past first base. Ignoring Wyatt's taunts, she focused on her swing, and on her next attempt, succeeded in cracking one between Billy and the Redcoats' first baseman, Elliot.

The hit was shallow enough for Elton not to catch the ball, but still enable him to pick up the ball and throw it to first before Farrow got there. Though she could hear Billy's smug laughter, Farrow smirked.

Bree had made it to second unencumbered, right where Farrow had intended to get her.

She saw Andrew give Bree the signal to steal if she could even as he looked at the next batter, Eddie. It was risky, but the element of surprise was on their side. Bree took a short lead so as not get picked off, waited until Denny let go of the ball to bullet toward third.

Eddie did his best to distract Wyatt by swinging at the pitch and missing, his body and his bat getting in Wyatt's way. He had to step around Eddie to throw to third, but by the time he did, Bree had already slid to safety and was standing.

Ryder didn't miss how Willoughby raked his eyes over Bree's dirt-clad bottom; even as he clenched his fists, Levi clapped a hand on his shoulder.

"She can handle herself."

"I know she can," Ryder grumbled. "Doesn't mean I have to like it."

Eddie struck out, but Fred, their cleanup hitter, took his time at the plate, before finally taking a hard swing and sending the ball deep into left field. Bree breezed over the plate, while Fred rounded first to see Thorpe had yet to reach the ball, and headed for second, where Andrew instructed him to stay.

Henry was the third out with an infield fly, but the Long-horns had scored the first run, which had them all grinning.

They managed to hold off the Redcoats in the bottom half of the inning, but were held off themselves in the top of the fourth, despite their best efforts. It seemed the Redcoats had deter-mined to play a little harder, and the roughness with which they were running and tagging runners didn't go unnoticed by the ump. Wyatt was even issued a warning for giving Levi a shove with his shoulder on his way to third.

In spite of the rough play, the Longhorns were still up one-nothing at the top of the fifth.

Farrow glowered at Wyatt as she slid a helmet over her head, pulling on her batting gloves when Knight went to the plate. The cocky bastard thought he could intimidate them with roughhousing and snide remarks, but the Longhorns would never stoop to that level.

As if proving her point, Knight lived up to his chivalrous name by studiously ignoring the Redcoats' jeers and patiently awaiting the right pitch. His patience was rewarded when he whacked the ball well over Crawford's head; by the time Forster reached the ball, Knight was coming up on second.

Similarly, Manny frustrated the other team by working his count to full before finally being walked.

Two on, no outs, Farrow thought, taking a fortifying breath. Their chances for a run or two this inning were good, but she felt the need to prepare herself just in case. There was no doubt in her mind Wyatt would try to mess with her.

She headed to the plate as Bree took Manny's place on first, and decided to follow her teammates' examples by taking her time. She watched one ball and one strike go by in silence. Just as she was thinking she was surprised Wyatt hadn't attempted anything, he spoke to her as he threw the ball back to Denny, apparently not caring if the umpire heard.

"So, you never answered my question. Does Gemma miss me?"

He'd have to do better than that if his goal was to provoke her. "Decidedly not," she answered, then readied for the next pitch. Denny threw just a little high and outside, her favorite kind of pitch, but she let it go.

"Are you sure?" Wyatt asked her, standing. "She was all over me."

This time Farrow ignored him. She let the heat of rage wash over her and settle in her core. She was done with his games.

He really thought it would be so easy to get to her?

She'd spent most of her life being underestimated, and not just because of her gender. Her reserved nature and social awkwardness had too often been perceived as a weakness; she'd had to work harder than others to be perceived as capable because she wasn't an easygoing extrovert.

But it had also worked to her advantage. When people underestimated you, they tended not to expect you to best them.

So thinking, she adjusted her grip on the bat, calmly waited for the next pitch, her honed instincts telling her it was the right one even as it left the pitcher's hand.

She rotated, swung.

Though it felt light as air, the crack of the ball against her bat reverberated through her, knocking it high into right center.

As Wyatt cursed, she dropped the bat and ran, elation and adrenaline fueling her as she watched Forster and Elton run after the ball. She stepped on the corner of the bag as she rounded first, not even bothering to slow down. She pulled up when she reached second, taking a moment to glance back to the outfield.

Elton had reached the ball, and was now throwing to Crawford, who was covering second. But to her surprise, the throw went a little wild, and even though Crawford leapt for the ball, he still missed it.

The shouts and cheers of "Go, go, go!" from the dugout and the stands filled her ears as the wild ball went flying into left field. Bree had already pushed off third, sprinting toward home, but Thorpe came up on the missed throw quickly, so Farrow stayed on two.

She ignored the glares of the players around her, particularly Billy, instead beaming toward the Longhorns dugout, where Bree was jogging up and high-fiving the others. Levi met her eyes and grinned back at her.

Carrying the momentum of their hitting streak, Eddie hit a single that brought Farrow to third. And Fred hit a hard grounder toward second. All the runners took off, and Billy lobbed the ball to Crawford, who was ready at second, even as Wyatt, who'd thrown off his helmet, stood over home plate and waved his arms for the ball.

And instead of trying for a double play at first, Crawford hurled the ball to Wyatt. Farrow threw herself down to slide legs first just as Wyatt caught the ball. And she slid over the plate as he bent to tag her.

His sweep hit her hard in the ribs, and she let out an *oof* even as the ump spread his arms and called safe.

"What?" Wyatt demanded as he straightened. "I totally got her!"

He'd got her alright. Knocked the wind out of her.

"That's another warning for playing with unnecessary roughness," the ump told him.

Farrow coughed as she sat up. Levi, Ryder, and Andrew were already running toward her. Levi reached out his hands, pulled her up when she gripped them.

"Did he hurt you?" he asked, sliding a protective arm around her waist.

"If she can't take a little tag, she shouldn't play in this league," Wyatt sneered, even as his gaze honed in on Levi and Farrow.

Both Levi and Ryder opened their mouths, but Farrow held

up a hand. Wyatt was deliberately provoking them, and she wasn't having it. "I'm fine, really. Just need to catch my breath. Carry on."

She walked toward the dugout, pulling Levi with her.

Ryder glared holes into Wyatt, had the satisfaction of seeing him shrink back a little. "You watch yourself, Wyatt," he warned before following the others back to the dugout.

Levi made Farrow sit once they'd reached the dugout, and Bree handed her her water bottle.

"That dickhead," she muttered. "He totally sucker punched you."

"He did," Farrow acknowledged. "But it won't do him any good."

The interruption seemed to have brought the team's mood down a little; if it had been unclear before, there was no longer any doubt the Redcoats weren't playing nice, and their previous momentum was lost.

Henry managed another single, but Jackson hit a fly into center, which was caught. And though Ryder cracked the ball over Billy's furious head, loading up the bases, Levi's worry over Farrow caused him to strike out, leaving all the runners stranded.

Ryder knew his friend would be beating himself up for his distraction, but when he saw the shuttered look on Levi's face as he jogged off the field, he knew something was up. He stopped him just outside the dugout.

"What did he say to you?" he asked in a low voice, pulling off his helmet.

Fury leapt into Levi's eyes, his jaw set. He glanced behind him to make sure Farrow wasn't paying attention; when he saw she was putting the catcher's gear on, he turned back to Ry. "Let's just say it was a crude comment about mine and Farrow's sex life. Don't tell Ro."

Ryder's eyes narrowed. "How would he…?"

"My reaction to his dirty play probably gave us away."

Ryder nodded. "It doesn't matter. The best way to stick it to him is to put it out of our minds."

Despite an overall great at-bat—they'd scored three runs and were now up four to nothing after all—the mood had soured.

Though her side ached a bit, Farrow didn't let it deter her. If anything, it was a point of pride to remain The Vac. A glance at the Redcoats' dugout at the end of the inning showed Wyatt's unmistakably annoyed face when his team failed to bring in any runs.

The Longhorns didn't get any runs in their next at-bat either.

Levi hoped he wasn't jinxing it when he reminded himself they were winning four to zero.

His hopes were for naught, however, as the Redcoats rallied in the bottom of the sixth. They were at the top of their rotation, so Thorpe led off, and got on base, followed by Elliot, who hit a single. With two on and no outs, it wasn't looking great, but Denny, thankfully, hit the ball right toward Knight, who scooped it up and stepped on third.

Unfortunately, Willoughby was next, and his hit brought Elliot in. Levi's senses pricked when Crawford sidled up to the plate, that baseball instinct that told him to be ready.

Crawford connected on the first pitch, sending a liner up the middle. Levi sprinted for it, reaching his arm as he dived, determined it wouldn't make it to the outfield—and to his delighted pleasure, the ball caught in the webbing of his glove.

He hit the ground with a jolt, heard the roar of cheers through the ringing in his ears. He rolled up, reaching into his glove for the ball as he glanced around to note the positions of the runners. Instead his eyes landed on Bree, who stood ready at nearby second, her eyes wide as her gloveless hand waved for him to throw her the ball.

Still on his knees, he tossed it to her, and she caught it easily, well before Denny, who'd made it all the way to third before he realized Levi had caught the ball, was able to return to second.

"Holy shit, dude." Ryder clamped his hand in Levi's as he helped him up. "That was the most epic thing I've ever seen."

"I'm glad you think so, 'cause I'll probably be feeling it tomorrow."

Ry just chuckled, and Levi grimaced a little as he walked it off. At least it was one hell of a play.

EIGHT

SADLY, they didn't get any runs in their next at bat either, and to make matters worse, the dreaded Forster was leading off for the Redcoats. Though he'd yet to get on base, he'd hit the ball every time, and this time was no exception.

To the Longhorns' dismay, he earned himself a triple when he smashed the ball into far right field. The next batter, Sanderson, hit the ball right to Henry, who had only to step on the bag for the out, but the hit still allowed Forster to score.

It wasn't all bad, though. Ryder struck out the next batter looking—poor Hurst, who was batting for Elton, had no idea what hit him—and the next batter was Billy.

Billy was always a wildcard batter. He often struck out, because his tendency was to swing at any pitch he though he could hit; but when he got lucky and connected, he usually got the ball into the outfield.

Such was the case in this instance; though it was shallow, he managed to hit it far enough over Henry's head to earn him a single.

That meant Wyatt was next at bat.

Though the looks he sent Farrow and Ryder could cut steel, he said nothing to them, and after swinging and missing a couple times, he too got lucky, sending the ball into left field. Fred got to the ball relatively quickly, and threw it to Knight, but Billy was called safe at third.

Ryder would have been happy to pick either of them off, but figured it would be better to focus on Thorpe. In his experience with the guy, he'd noticed he had more confidence than skill, but he wasn't to be underestimated.

Cockiness did sometimes lend one a certain amount of power.

This estimation was proven when Thorpe sent the ball sailing high into center field. It wasn't terribly deep, so both runners kept careful watch, and when Jackson easily caught the ball, Wyatt went back to first.

Billy though, tagged up and decided he could make it home.

It seemed he'd forgotten why Jackson was such a good center fielder. Instead of throwing the ball to Levi, or to Ryder, Jackson launched the ball to home plate.

Farrow had tossed her mask aside, and stood with her legs on either side of the plate, ready for the throw. Knowing Billy, she anticipated he might knock into her, so when she caught the ball, she turned to face him, glove closed in front of her with both hands, bending her legs to absorb his impact just before he rammed into her.

Though she shoved against his chest, he succeeded in knocking her over. She clutched her glove to her chest as she turned her body to brace for the fall, while Billy practically did a tap dance on home plate.

"You're out!" The umpire called.

"What?!" Billy roared, turning on him. "Are you blind? She didn't hold on to the ball!"

"I did, actually." Though Ryder and Levi had rushed to help her up, Farrow was already standing, opening her glove to reveal the ball. "And I tagged you as you ran into me."

"For which I'll have to issue you a warning," the ump said,

his face stern and unmoving. "Any more foul play from you, and you're outta here. Understand?"

Billy's face was red with indignation, and he looked like he wanted to tear the ump a new one, but he nodded before stomping back to the Redcoats' dugout.

"Are you okay?" Ryder asked Ro as they walked back to their own dugout.

"I'll probably be sore tomorrow, but I'm fine," she said, rubbing a hand over her butt. "Now, there's two innings left and we're ahead by two. The sooner we hold them off, the sooner we can go have a celebratory beer."

"Amen to that."

To their surprise—although, perhaps it shouldn't have been surprising—Billy replaced Denny as the Redcoats' pitcher. Sanderson now stood at second.

Billy was a decent pitcher, but like his batting, his pitching tended to be a little wild. Henry hit the ball into left, but Thorpe made the catch. Jackson waited Billy out, but eventually hit a line drive that Sanderson snagged.

When he got to the plate, Ryder thought he'd mix it up with a little switch hitting; it would have the added benefit of taunting Billy a bit.

He let a few pitches go by. One of them was a strike—barely —and he smirked at Billy. Perhaps he should have been warned by the cold hatred in Billy's eyes, but that was the other thing about wildcards.

They tended to surprise you.

He knew the ball was going to hit him when it reached the halfway point; he turned his body inward, away from the ball, but it still hit him.

Right in the arm.

Pain exploded, the senses in his arm turned sharp and blistering before settling into a dull but poignant ache. He had no idea if he made any sound, but he heard the bat hit the ground as he gripped his arm.

As Andrew rushed over, Levi rushed from his position on deck to his friend, glaring into Billy's smug face. Before he could ask Ryder if he was alright, the ump glowered at Billy.

"You're OUTTA HERE!" He barked, pumping his arm in the universal motion for "out."

"You can't do that!" Billy yelled back, then pointed at Andrew. "He said something to you, didn't he?"

"Son, if you think I can't tell you did that on purpose, you're mistaken. Pack your bags."

Irate, Billy threw his glove down on the mound. "Fuck you! Fuck all of you!" he declared, then swiped up his glove and marched into the dugout. He cursed the whole time he shoved gear into his bag, but Levi paid him no mind.

"Doesn't he know there's no crying in baseball?" he said to a chuckling Ry, laying a hand on his shoulder before asking, "Are you okay?"

"Yeah," Ryder gritted through his teeth. "I'll probably have a mother of a bruise, though."

He shook out his arm as if to shake away the pain, but it only served to prove to him how sore he already was. When he looked to the dugout to see all his teammates watching, and Bree's eyes glinting with unshed tears, he nodded to Levi and Andrew. "Let's finish this."

He jogged to first, gave Bree a smile so she knew he was alright, and focused on the game. Denny, of course, came back to the mound; he worked Levi to a full count.

Levi knew he was distracted. First, Farrow had been hurt—twice—and now Ryder's pitching arm was in jeopardy. Although Billy getting thrown out of the game was a highlight, he couldn't help thinking things would get worse before they got better.

He was frustrated with himself for thinking it, for doubting himself and his team, on top of his worry for Farrow and Ry.

He didn't strike out, but he did hit a grounder to short,

where it was easily scooped up by Crawford, who stepped on two for the last out.

"Ryder," Bree said to him when he entered the dugout, her voice shaky.

"I'm fine, baby," he assured her.

"Fine or not, you're not pitching this inning." Andrew folded his arms, gave his cousin his no-nonsense look. "Knight will go in for you while you rest your arm. Eddie will take third."

Though he frowned, Ryder nodded.

"Ry." On the other side of the fence next to the dugout, Tina held up a bag of ice. Ro stepped out of the dugout, caught it when Tina tossed it over, handed it to Ry. He took it and placed it over the red welt on his arm, took a seat on the bench as the others went out to take their positions.

"Thanks, Tina," he said to her. "That was quick thinking."

"Ro asked me to run to the concession stand for it." She shrugged, smiled. "But you're welcome."

Farrow didn't know Knight's movements as well as she knew Ryder's, but he was a good pitcher. Steady, dependable. She and Ry had worked with him more after Billy quit, and he'd improved substantially.

His newness was also an advantage in that the other team had yet to get used to him. Farrow thought maybe their luck was picking back up when they got three up, three down; out of the three Redcoats batters—Elliot, Denny, and Willoughby— only Denny had gotten a hit.

Her opinion didn't change when Brandon and Knight both got on base in the top of the ninth; though Manny was thrown out at first, Denny showed some of his nerves by pitching her four balls in a row.

With the bases loaded, Eddie came up to the plate. Unfortunately, he hit an infield fly, called and caught by Denny. Fred faired better, smashing the ball into center, but it was, of course, caught by Forster.

It was disappointing, but what was even more disappointing was the realization that the Redcoats' big hitters were next in the line up.

"At least they're first, so there won't be too many runners on base when Forster demolishes the ball," Manny mumbled, scuffing his cleat against the cement floor of the dugout.

"Hey," Ryder protested. "The game's not over yet. And we're still winning."

Fred rolled his eyes. "Well, now you've jinxed it."

"Come on, you guys. Ryder's right," Levi said quietly. "All we have to do is hold them back for three more outs."

Though they all agreed, Levi wasn't sure he'd convinced everyone, himself included.

Perhaps that was why Crawford hit a double after fouling one off. And when Forster stepped up to bat, Levi could have sworn clouds rolled in, and even the sun wanted to hide.

He didn't demolish the ball, exactly, but he did slam it far enough that it bounced against the back right field fence. Crawford, of course, had no problem scoring, Forster landed himself another triple, and the Longhorns' lead dwindled to one.

Sanderson followed that up by hitting the ball into right field as well; this was caught by Brandon, but Forster tagged up before heading for home.

The score was tied.

The next two hitters were easily dispatched. Hurst, who swung lazily at pitches, struck out, while Elton, who hadn't batted all game but now had to replace Billy in the lineup, hit a grounder to Eddie at third and was thrown out at first.

But the damage was done. They'd have to go into extra innings.

"Alright, you guys," Andrew said when they shuffled into the dugout. "I know this has been a hard game, but we need to pull it back out for just a little longer."

"I know we just gave up a couple runs," Jackson stated. "But if they can come back, so can we. All we need is one run, and we're back on top. We can rally."

Nodding, Andrew continued, "We play it smart. Our primary goal is to get runners on base; try to hit the ball where they can't easily field it."

The team looked around at each other, faces still quiet and solemn. Inside, Farrow's emotions were roiling. She was tired and battered, and stupid Greg Wyatt was smirking at them as he walked up to the plate. He gave them the middle finger as he pulled his mask down over his face.

"We want a rally," she murmured.

"What?" Bree turned to her, though her slow smile told Farrow she'd probably heard, and Farrow smiled back.

"We want a rally," she said louder, her voice turning sing-song.

Bree gave the ground one hard stomp as she followed up with, "Just a little rally!"

"Oh, for…" Fred muttered, but his eye-roll went unnoticed by the two friends as their cheer picked up momentum.

"We want a rally, rally, rally, rally, just a little rally, rally, rally, rally!"

In the stands, Tina, Cat, and Nora jumped up from the seats and joined in the chant. They repeated it a couple more times, more and more of the fans joining in each time. Even Frank and the Bennet brothers added their voices. When they stopped and those in the bleachers let out some hurrahs of support, Farrow turned back to the team and their now amused faces.

"We can do this," she said simply. "I know we can."

"I'm still looking forward to that celebratory beer," Henry said, grinning and grabbing up a batting helmet.

"Me, too." Levi kept his eyes on Farrow's as he leaned against the fencing. "So let's make sure we get it."

Sufficiently roused, Henry, Jackson, and Ryder got ready to bat.

"You gonna be able to swing okay?" Ro asked Ryder as Levi came to stand beside her.

"It's sore, but I'll manage," Ryder answered, eyeing her. "You doing okay?"

Farrow sighed, allowing her eyes to drift to Wyatt again. "He stole something from me that I loved, and until recently, I thought I'd never get it back. I'll be damned if I'll let him take it again."

"He won't," Levi assured her, then thought of their words the night before and repeated, "I believe that."

She smiled, slid her hand into his. "So do I."

He did believe it, Levi thought. The Longhorns were the better team, and they knew how to be one. He'd struggled not to let Billy and Wyatt's antics get to him, but there was nothing either could do or say to him now. Farrow's strong hand squeezing his only reinforced that belief.

And he wasn't the only one who seemed to have gotten his groove back. Henry, cheeky soul that he was, let a couple pitches go by before crouching to bunt at the last second.

The ball rolled a little ways up the third base line, Denny, Willoughby, and Wyatt all scrambling after it while Henry booked it to first. It was Willoughby who reached the ball first, but Henry reached the bag several seconds before the ball.

Laughing, Levi readied himself as Jackson took the plate.

Jackson seemed to have a plan in mind as well. When he swung and missed, Levi noticed he wasn't swinging as hard as he usually did. On his next swing, Jackson knocked the ball over Denny's head high enough he couldn't reach it, and it landed in shallow center, where Forster had to come up on it. Henry made it safely to two, and Jackson to one.

Then it was Ryder's turn.

Some of the Redcoats were smirking, probably expecting he wouldn't swing very hard, and some even moved in a little.

Levi took some testing swings in time with Denny's pitches as Ryder worked his count to full. Then, when the final pitch appeared to be a strike, Ryder surprised even his own team by bunting just as Henry had.

This time the ball went toward first, so Elliot ran up for it while Sanderson covered first. They threw Ryder out, but both Henry and Jackson had advanced a base.

Levi blew out a breath as he came around the plate to the right side. All he had to do was hit the ball into the outfield, and Henry, maybe even Jackson, could score.

Easy-peasy.

"Levi."

He turned to Andrew, who gave him the new sign for swing away. He nodded, then stepped into the batter's box.

The first pitch was a ball. As with his last at-bat, Wyatt whispered to him as he returned the ball to Denny.

"Ro can really take a hit, huh? I bet she likes it rough."

Levi'd be damned if he dignified that with a response. Wyatt only chuckled when Levi said nothing, but if he said anything else, Levi had tuned him out. He let the next pitch go by, even though it was a strike. He had a feeling the next one was his.

And it was.

It was one of those moments where you just know, and time seems to slow for you even though it doesn't feel slow at all; and Denny had the decency to throw the ball right down the heart of the plate.

Levi swung, and the ball hit the sweet spot; the resounding *crack* of hard leather against wood echoed in his ears as the ball flew into left field. He'd just rounded first when the cheers reached his ears, and he realized the ball had dropped on the other side of the fence.

He slowed his pace and jogged around the horn, a little in a daze. Andrew slapped him on the back as he rounded third, and when his feet touched home plate it finally hit him.

He'd just hit a home run. A three-run homer. In the championship game.

He re-entered the dugout to the grins and backslaps of his

teammates. Bree squealed as she hugged him, and Farrow gave him a look of such heat as she approached him, Levi thought his insides would melt.

She stopped in front of him, tilted her face up to look into his eyes as her lips curved. "Good job, Slugger."

He quirked a brow. "Do I get a victory kiss?"

"Mm." Amusement filled her sultry blue eyes. "Ask me again when the game is over."

The rally wasn't over yet.

Brandon slammed one into right, earning him an easy single; Knight slid a grounder into left between short and third, advancing himself and Brandon.

But the streak ended when Manny hit a liner right between first and second. Sanderson caught it, and tagged out Knight, who hadn't yet had time to turn around for first.

None of this deterred from their good mood, though, Farrow noticed as she moved quickly to put the catcher's gear back on. She had to admit she was a little relieved not to bat again.

"What are you doing?" she asked Ryder when she saw him grab up his glove.

"My arm is better," he said, stretching it a little. "The ice helped a lot."

She only gave him a bland look.

"Don't give me that, Vac," he said. "Wyatt's up next, and I'm going to strike him out if it's the last thing I do in this game."

"If he says he can pitch, I say let him," Knight said. "I'll sit this one out."

"Are you sure?" Andrew asked him.

Knight shrugged. "I kind of just want to watch the magic happen."

"Then let's make it happen." Ryder grinned. "Three up, three down."

Ryder threw several warm up pitches, each one getting harder and faster. You'd hardly know he'd taken a fastball to his pitching arm, Farrow thought—that is, until you noticed the bruise forming on that arm.

She imagined they'd all be a little bruised after this game. But it would be worth it for the reminder of how hard they'd fought to win.

A few feet away, Wyatt was taking some practice swings.

"Do I sense Torch's flame going out?" he called to Ryder.

"I've got enough left to burn you," Ryder said without looking at him, then threw a blazer smack into Farrow's glove to prove it. She felt the sting against her hand and relished in it.

Sure of himself, Wyatt only smirked.

When he stepped into the batter's box, the death glares he and Ryder exchanged made her think of a wild west duel, heard the flute melody and *'wah, wah, wah,'* in her head, and smiled under her mask.

Ryder proved to be the faster shooter when he threw a tidy slider, and Wyatt swung and whiffed the air. Growling, Wyatt swung harder at the next pitch, a change up, as though that would make his aim more accurate.

It wasn't.

Wyatt's nostrils flared. If he was smart, he'd have let that pitch go by, Farrow thought. But all he seemed capable of focusing on at the moment was his vendetta against her and Ryder.

Farrow gave Ryder a sign, but he shook his head. She chose another and he nodded, a hint of a smirk on his lips.

Ah. So he wanted to give Wyatt a pitch he wouldn't be able to resist.

Ryder wound up, hitched his leg, and let the ball fly. From the onset it looked like a perfect fastball, just a little outside. And when Wyatt rotated, swung, the ball curved inward, slapping into Farrow's glove near the inside corner of the plate.

"Strike three!" called the ump.

"No!" Wyatt shouted, and heaved his bat to the ground.

Farrow threw the ball back to Ryder, stood hipshot as she cocked her head at her old foe.

"Didn't you know you shouldn't play with fire, Wyatt?" she quipped.

"Argh!" was all he could say, and he kicked the bat toward his dugout. The next batter, Thorpe, eyed him as they passed each other, and Farrow thought she heard him say something like, "Dude, chill."

Thorpe nearly struck out, too. But unlike Wyatt, he calmed himself to let a ball go by before swinging again. And when he did, he hit a low liner toward third. Instead of coming up on it in an attempt to catch it, Eddie stayed back; when the ball hit the ground at an angle, bounced up, he snatched it up, threw it to first.

Only one out to go, Farrow thought, and it's in the bag. She was sure the rest of her team was thinking the same thing; she could practically feel their excitement buzzing like a current. Out of her peripheral, she could see Knight and Manny standing in the dugout, watching intently, and their friends and family in the stands starting to cheer for them.

Elliot had more patience than the first two batters. He waited out balls, and when he swung, he nicked the ball a couple times, fouling them back. When he reached a full count, everyone on and off the field went silent, almost as if holding a collective breath.

Ryder went through the motions, threw.

Elliot pivoted, swung.

She heard the bat meet the ball, but didn't see the ball anywhere. It took her a second, but as she heard the cheers erupt, she realized he'd fouled the ball right into her waiting glove; and sure enough, when she looked down at her mitt, the ball had nestled itself inside.

"Yeah!"

She paid no mind to the other team as she jumped up, yanking off her glove and mask and letting them drop to the ground. Ryder was already running to meet her when she moved as fast as her shin guard-clad legs could go, and jumped into his waiting arms.

She laughed as he spun her around, the rest of the team joining in the victory party. When Ryder set Farrow on her feet, he immediately turned and grabbed up Levi in a bear hug, while Bree came up and threw her arms around Farrow.

And then, finally, she was facing a beaming Levi.

"How 'bout that kiss?" he asked.

He'd only gotten about halfway through the question before she gripped the front of his jersey, tugged him to her. His arms came around her shoulders as their lips met in a perfect, heady kiss.

When they parted, looked around, they saw everyone else was still engaged in their own celebration. Tina was hugging Jackson, Cat had found Henry, and Bree and Ryder in particular were still embracing. Frank was hooting and hollering with his team, pumping his now cast-free arm in the air. Farrow and Levi only grinned at each other as his other brothers surrounded them, clapped them on the back.

"Hey!" Andrew finally called above the ruckus, whistled for their attention. When they all turned to find him standing at home plate with a trophy the size of his torso, he smiled and held it up.

"I think you all earned that beer."

EPILOGUE

Six Months Later

PEOPLE MILLED through the brightly lit rooms, winter sunshine shimmering through the big, clear windows. Bits of color from the original stained glass tops added charm as they commented and exclaimed over the designs and craftsmanship, trying to decide which was their favorite. They sipped champagne out of crystal flutes and nibbled on appetizers as they discussed possible reasons to book a room—anniversary gift topped the list—while others were determined to book the parlor rooms for their bridal or baby shower, their book club, an afternoon tea party, a birthday, or even a wedding.

Farrow stood with Bree and Ryder in the foyer, resplendent in a blue floral dress, observing it all. It was heartening and extremely satisfying to see all their hard work come to fruition, in an abundance of ways.

It had been touch and go for some moments. Renovations were always a little fraught, but only a couple of months after she and Levi started seeing each other, her parents had offered her a position heading up the Pemberley offices in New York.

That had been the hardest moment.

Not with her and Levi—though what they had was still new, she hadn't questioned it. No, the hard part was telling her family she didn't want it. And not only that, she wanted to do something outside of Pemberley.

They'd been upset, but not for the reasons she thought they'd be. They understood why she didn't want to move halfway across the country, and even why she wanted to explore her options. They'd only felt guilty she hadn't felt like she could talk to them about what she wanted.

Well, Uncle Lewis didn't understand at all. He thought everything she was doing was a mistake—especially her relationship with Levi. But no one—not even Andrew—cared what he thought.

In the end, not only had she stayed in Chicago, she'd decided to partner with Bree, and they'd made the Netherfield Inn their own. Bree's designs for each room were cozy, and seamlessly blended the building's antique roots with modern touches.

Her own hospitality knowledge allowed her to explore ideas for room packages, services, hosting events, and other behind-the-scenes nuances that wouldn't work at Pemberley, but which would make a suburban B&B shine.

And now they watched, soaking it all in, as they unveiled their baby to the community.

The Bennets were all in attendance, of course, as was her own family (except Uncle Lewis). Landon and Kyle mingled easily, talking to guests about the renovation, while Mason seemed to have been chosen as the chaperone for Mrs. Bennet—the one charged with keeping her from approaching young ladies in order to introduce them to her sons.

He wasn't entirely alone in his efforts; Andrew, as the lone representative of the Dubois family, kept him company. Since his father did not approve, he'd doubled his efforts to show his support, and Farrow appreciated his presence more than he knew.

She couldn't see where Mr. Bennet had gotten to—though she had a suspicion—but she did spot Jackson, all cozied up in the corner by the fireplace with Tina.

Now there was a heartwarming story, she thought. The two would-be lovers; one, caught in a love triangle, the other overlooked. He, realizing his heart had been in front of him all along, and she coming to understand she'd thought herself in love with the wrong brother.

Tina was moving in with Jackson over the weekend, but they weren't kicking Levi out.

Mostly because he'd already moved in to her place a couple weeks ago. Rearranging the bookshelves to fit his books in with hers had been an interesting exercise of their patience, but also a unique bonding experience. Even now it made her smile.

As did the memory of the one and only time she'd beaten him at Mario Party.

They'd invited the whole team, too. All the guys had come, bringing their current or prospective partners along. She and Bree had made the rounds to all of them, and had a particularly enjoyable conversation with Nora Dashwood, who'd come with Eddie.

She knew Nora had dated Levi once upon a time, but it was really hard to be jealous when Nora was so sweet. And though she and Levi were still friends, her eyes were clearly only for Eddie. Farrow liked her immensely, and already counted her a friend.

She knew Ryder's parents, her parents, and her sister were around somewhere, as well, networking. Her mother loved networking (Farrow did not), and Gemma was shaping up to be the sociable one.

As for her father...now that she thought about it, it had been a while since she'd seen him. Maybe she should—

Grinning, Ryder slung one arm over Bree's shoulders, the other over Farrow's.

"If you build it, they will come," he said, proudly looking around at all the guests.

"He will come," Farrow corrected.

"What?"

"The line is, 'If you build it, *he* will come.' I know grammatically 'they' is appropriate for this situation, but that's one of the most misquoted lines in movie history."

Amused, Ryder shook his head, gave her a squeeze. "You just had to correct me, didn't you?"

"Yes, I did," Farrow acknowledged with a teasing smile.

Just then, Levi came around the corner with Bree's brother. He looked incredibly handsome in a pair of light brown corduroy pants and a burnt orange button down shirt, and she used the opportunity to run admiring eyes over him. He was nodding politely to whatever Brody was saying, his expression blank, like his eyes were glazing over, but when he glanced up and saw her, his face brightened and warmed.

He kept his soft gray eyes on hers as he approached them, spread his arms to gesture around the room.

"I think it's a hit."

Moving away from Ryder and exchanging his arm for Levi's, Farrow beamed. "We're not even officially open yet, and we're already booked solid for the next month."

Brody observed the couple with a curled lip, but reserved a particularly gimlet eye for Levi's arm around Farrow's shoulders, lifted his chin a little.

"Undoubtedly this will become *the* place for high society events and clientele," he said.

Nodding, Farrow slid her arm around Levi's waist. "We want everyone to be able to stay and plan events here, not just high society. But Mom's already talking about hosting the annual charity gala here."

Bree's eyes widened. "Isn't that soon? She doesn't mean this year, right?"

"Thankfully, no—they booked the venue for this year's event last year."

Bree let out an audible *whew*, and a chuckling Ryder pressed a kiss to her forehead.

"Have you seen my dad?" Farrow asked Levi. "I was going to go look for him."

"Both our fathers are hiding out in the library with a whole bottle of champagne," he told her.

"Ugh, no fair," she pouted. "Why can't I hide in the library?"

"Because this is your open house party," he chuckled, and tapped her nose. "As you well know."

Bree's eyes went soft. "You two are too cute."

Brody made an inexplicable noise of disgust, and turned on his heel, heading toward the refreshment table.

"Ignore him." Bree waved a hand. "He's always cranky."

That was putting it mildly, Farrow thought. Brody had never been the warmest person, but since he'd found out she was with Levi, he'd become positively frigid. She'd known he'd gotten it in his head she should date *him*, but though he'd tried to impress her, his methods proved he didn't understand her at all.

The fact she was interested in someone he considered beneath him only made him dislike Levi all the more. It was unfortunate—mostly for Levi—but it hardly mattered.

As if proving just why he was perfect for her, Levi dropped his arm and tugged at her hand. "Come on. Let's go see if we can join the party in the library."

She smiled widely. "I'm already there."

Nodding to Bree and Ryder, they made their way up the wide staircase, passing other guests on their way down from exploring the rooms.

"This place is a dream!" one Farrow recognized an acquaintance of her mother's gushed.

"Thank you." She automatically smiled the polite, friendly smile she'd adapted for social situations.

It took them a few minutes to get to the library, as they spoke to a few more guests on the way. When they rounded the corner to find their fathers sitting in the pair of plush armchairs, the two men looked up from their discussion with welcoming and slightly tipsy smiles.

"Hello, darling. Are you here to join us?" her father asked.

"We are," she replied, eyeing the bottle of champagne and extra glasses on the coffee table as she and Levi sat on the velvet sofa. "I hope you saved some champagne for us."

"There's plenty to go around, my dear," said Mr. Bennet, lifting the bottle and pouring some into a glass for each of them.

"You knew we'd come find you," Levi mused, taking his glass.

"We had a hunch."

Farrow took her own glass, savored a sip. "How long do you think until Mom notices we're not mingling downstairs?"

Her father blew out a breath. "Oh, probably not long."

"Then we'd better make the most of it." Levi said, and held up his glass for a toast. "To the Netherfield Inn."

Farrow raised her glass. "To the family that restored it."

"To the brilliant women who own it," Levi added.

"To this library," said Mr. Bennet.

Her father spoke through their laughter. "Here, here."

They clinked their glasses, were just taking their celebratory sips when her mother came around the corner, placed her hands on her hips when she spotted them.

"I should have known you'd be up here. You know there's a perfectly good party going on downstairs?"

"Yes, Dear," her father smiled. "And it's doing just fine without us."

Her mother gave him an indulgent smile. "You perhaps, but Farrow dear, Mrs. Annesley is looking for you."

"Of course she is." Resigned, Farrow set down her glass, stood. "Back into the fray."

"I'll come with you," Levi told her.

"No, you stay. Enjoy the library."

"Ro." He ignored her protest and rose. "I'm coming with you."

"Alright."

His insistence on accompanying her was just another reason she loved him, and his presence as they interacted with more guests helped her settle into her role as hostess.

And at the end of the night, when they'd ushered the last of the guests out the door and only family remained, Levi pulled Farrow back to the library, which was blessedly empty, to take a breath.

"Why is socializing so exhausting?" she sighed, sinking onto the window seat cushion.

"It takes focus and energy." Levi sat next to her, rubbed her shoulders in comfort. "But soon we'll be able to go home and curl up in bed, just the two of us."

She turned and, giving him the coy smile she knew he loved, she ran her hands over his chest. "Sooner than that. I may have secured the penthouse suite for us tonight."

His brow lifted, just the way she liked it. "Oh, really?"

"Mm-hm." She pressed a quick kiss to his lips.

"Have I told you I love you?"

Grinning, she pulled back to take his hands. "You may have."

His gaze softened, the way it did only when he looked at her. "Well I do."

"Good," she murmured, leaning in to him. "Because I love you."

"And you still know how to throw me curveballs."

She smirked. "Good curveballs, I hope."

He nodded, cupped her face, and before laying his lips on hers, murmured, "This one went right down the heart."

PLAYER INDEX

THE LONGHORNS

Levi Bennet (SS)
Jackson Bennet (CF)
Farrow "The Vac" Darcy (C)
Ryder "Torch" Williams (P)
Andrew Dubois (Coach)
Henry North (1st)
Leo Knight (3rd or P)
Brandon Coleman (RF)
Fred Rakowski (LF)
Eddie Fernandez (LF or 3rd)
Manny Bertolli (RF or 1st)
Billy Collins (2nd or P)

Alternate Players

Frank Chopra (C)
Bree Carpenter (2nd)

THE REDCOATS

Greg Wyatt
Denny
Forster
Sanderson
Thorpe
Willoughby
Crawford
Elton
Elliot
Hurst

Alternate Players

Billy Collins

BONUS SCENE

Want more Bree and Ryder? Keep reading for a special bonus scene, and find out what happened when our would-be lovers finally confessed their feelings to each other...

⁂

SHE WAS A TERRIBLE person.

Oh, God. She was the most terrible, horrible...terrible person on the planet.

In the middle of her bright, sunny kitchen, Bree paced, a storm cloud rolling in as she scolded herself over and over. She couldn't shake the guilt, or her jittery fear as she waited for the one person who made her simultaneously giddy and frustrated.

The guilt came from turning down Jackson Bennet when he'd asked her out.

Poor, sweet, kindhearted Jackson, she thought, her face crumpling. She genuinely enjoyed his company—and it didn't hurt that he was easy on the eyes. She hadn't intentionally led him on, but she hadn't discouraged the quiet attention he'd paid her either. Now she was dealing with the fallout of that.

Not that there was much fallout. Jackson had taken it well. And when she'd felt like she needed to explain herself, her feelings, he'd understood.

Of course he'd understood; he was Jackson Bennet, the epitome of the nice guy. A more deserving man she'd never met. Why couldn't she fall in love with him instead?

She stopped her pacing, huffed to herself.

Because she was already stupidly in love with stupid Ryder Williams.

Which was what she'd explained to Jackson. She was in love with Ryder, and had been for years. She was just too afraid to say anything to him.

But her best friend Ro, who also happened to be Ryder's cousin, had convinced her she couldn't stand by and do nothing anymore, so she was going to do it. Somehow, she was going to work up the courage to tell Ryder how she felt.

That was a week ago.

She'd let a whole week go by after she'd talked to Jackson, and asked him not to say anything about her feelings. Now that she'd dragged him into it, it wasn't fair to keep him guessing, constantly watching her with concern in his eyes.

Enough was enough. It was time to man up, so to speak, which was why she'd texted Ryder and asked him to come over. Why she was walking back and forth as she waited, trying to figure out what she was going to say—because of course she hadn't put any thought into it during the week she'd procrastinated.

She pressed a hand to her stomach as butterflies beat their wings against their cage.

The buzzer sounded, sending more nerves skittering under her skin. She found herself at her front door without remembering the steps to get there, pressed the intercom button in a daze.

"Hello?"

Was that her voice? She sounded like a robot.

"Hey, it's Ry."

"Okay." She pressed the button to let him in, hoped against hope she could eke out more than one word at a time.

She waited what felt like an inconceivably long time before his knock came, and she flung the door open so fast, his fist was still raised to knock again, and his blue eyes widened on her face. She didn't know what she looked like, but she'd obviously startled him, so she worked to school her features.

"Thanks for coming," she blurted, then remembered she was blocking the entrance and stepped aside for him to come in.

"Uh, no problem." Ryder eyed her warily. "Everything okay?"

That's a loaded question, she thought, closing the door.

When she looked over at him, saw he'd cocked an eyebrow at her, she realized she hadn't answered him.

"Yeah, yeah. Everything's….going."

His expression turned skeptical. "Everything's going."

"Yep!" she said, too brightly, twisting her fingers together.

"Bree, should I be worried?" He moved a little closer to her, stilled her fidgeting movements with a hand to her shoulder. "Why did you ask me to come over?"

She was losing her nerve, damn it.

How many more years of suffering unrequited love would she put herself through because she just couldn't get the words out?

The answer will always be no if you never ask.

Ro's words rang in her ears, ricocheting around like a cartoon character who'd been hit on the head.

"Bree?"

Ryder was looking at her intently now, concern etched in the narrowing of his eyes, in the lines of his normally cheerful face.

She took a deep, gulping breath to steady herself. "Because I need to talk to you."

"What about?"

"You might want to sit down for this."

She moved back from him, gestured toward the kitchen. She needed him not to be touching her; she didn't know if she could get out what she needed to tell him if he was so close.

"Okay…"

Clearly still concerned, Ryder stepped ahead of her into the kitchen, took a seat at the table. His concern and confusion only deepened when, instead of sitting with him, Bree began to pace.

She knew she was disconcerting him, but really, it shouldn't surprise him that she couldn't sit still. That was usually the case, anyway.

Once again, he broke the unnerving silence. "Are you going to tell me what it is you want to talk about?"

"Yes," she said absently, allowing herself one more round of pacing before halting and breathing out, "Okay. Ryder."

He pursed his lips. "Bree."

"I have something to tell you."

Concern softened into familiar amusement. "Yet, you have yet to actually tell me what that something is."

She huffed. "It's not quite that easy."

"Isn't it?" He quirked a brow, reminding her of his cousin. "You just put one word after the other until you have a full sentence."

She was frustrated, but not with him. She was stalling, and she knew it. But his teasing was one of the things she loved about him, and it settled some of her nerves.

And since one of her favorite things was teasing him back, perhaps she should start there.

Pretending to be irked with him, she fisted her hands on her hips. "Oh, and I suppose if you were going to confess that you've been in love with me for years, you'd be perfectly confident, and eloquent, and charming."

His slightly amused, watchful expression slid slowly off his face, his jaw going slack, and something like fear flashing in his eyes.

He tried to laugh, but it came out strangled. "What?"

"I said, I suppose you'd be confident, eloquent, and charming if you were going to tell me you have feelings for me," she said simply, trying not to be dismayed by the stricken look on his face. "You wouldn't be afraid, and you'd know exactly what to say. So go on then."

Ro had told her, Ryder concluded, his mind spinning. She must have. He'd done so well at hiding his feelings, even Levi and Tina, his most perceptive friends, had never noticed.

And now, exactly what he was afraid would happen was happening. Bree was clearly not pleased, staring him down and…what, demanding he come clean? She couldn't be asking that of him. It would tilt the balance of their friendship considerably.

He cleared his throat before speaking slowly. "Go on then?"

"Tell me what I should say." It occurred to her she might not be making any sense, and endeavored to make herself clearer. "If you're so confident it's that simple, then tell me what to say, and I'll say it."

Relief warred with pain inside him. She didn't know; instead she seemed to be asking for help asking someone out.

And he thought he knew who that someone was.

He'd be damned if he'd stick around to listen to the woman he loved talk about her feelings for someone else, and aid her in doing so. That was too much.

Sighing, he rose from his seat, laid a hand on the back of the chair.

"Look, Bree, you don't have to be afraid."

Her soft green eyes rounded, warming with hope. "I don't?"

It killed him.

But her needs pulled at him more, so he gave her the assurance she needed, and nodded.

"There's no way Jackson would say no to you."

Her face fell so quickly it was almost comical.

"Jackson."

She said his friend's name in a bland, uncomprehending tone he'd never heard in her bell-bright voice before.

"Ye-es?" Suddenly he wasn't so sure.

And suddenly she stood straighter, more primly. "I'll have you know, Jackson already asked me out last week," she said, a little frostily. "And I turned him down."

"You…" Maybe his brain was short-circuiting, because if she hadn't meant Jackson, then… "Then who are you talking about?"

"You, you idiot!" She burst out, throwing up her hands. "I'm trying to tell you I'm in love with *you*. Lord knows why."

Actually, she did know why, but that was neither here nor there. She'd finally said the words, finally released a secret she'd held close for so long.

And it felt pretty good, despite the fact the object of her affection was standing there gaping at her.

Ryder was quite literally struck dumb.

She was talking about him. She was really talking about *him*. Those gorgeous lake green eyes were really, truly, looking at him with an exasperated affection he hadn't let himself see or acknowledge before.

He knew wholeheartedly she'd been wrong—he wasn't confident at all, not when it came to her. And obviously she was braver than he was, since she'd been the one to tell him of her feelings.

Ro was right, he thought to himself. She'd told him so many times he'd get what he wanted if he just took the chance and spoke to Bree.

But he'd been too afraid—afraid she wouldn't love him back, afraid to ruin their friendship, afraid to make things awkward between her and his cousin.

All of which seemed insignificant in the face of the over-whelming joy threatening to burst forth from his chest.

Bree's expression was shifting from exasperation to wari-ness, and Ryder realized he'd yet to respond to her bold confes-sion; she probably thought she was alone in her feelings.

No, that wasn't wariness, that was disappointment.

Well, if she could be brave, so could he.

"I—I don't expect you to return my feelings," Bree stuttered. "I just—"

"Bree." He spoke softly, stepped over to her.

"I just want—"

He laid a finger against her lips, allowing his face to show all the love and admiration he felt for her as he looked down into her welling eyes.

He swallowed, daring to trace his finger over her bottom lip, reveling in its softness. "I…" He intended to tell her in words, but at the moment they were deserting him.

"Fuck it."

He moved his hand to cup the back of her head, slid his other arm around her, and crushed his lips to hers, absorbing her intake of breath.

Her response was immediate and giving. She melted against him, fluid and torrential as water, wrapping her arms around his neck, deepening the already fierce kiss. She seemed to vibrate with light and energy and passion; he hugged his other arm around her, unwilling to let that light slip away.

She felt tingly everywhere.

Finally, *finally,* she was in Ryder's arms, and it was everything she'd imagined and more. He kissed her like he was drowning and she was air. Maybe he had been drowning the same way she had been.

Then, abruptly, he pulled back.

"I am an idiot," he said. His blue eyes had darkened with desire, and his arms tightened around her to keep her from moving away. "I'm so in love with you I can't even comprehend it, and I could've told you years ago."

"Why didn't you?"

"I *was* afraid. You were wrong about that."

A watery laugh escaped her as her eyes welled again. "We're both idiots. I've loved you for so long I barely remember being interested in anyone else. But I was afraid, too."

"Ro told me I should just tell you, you know," he confessed. "It's my own fault for not listening to her."

"Me, too—although this time I did listen to her." She closed her eyes, chuckling. "Oh, God, she's going to be so *smug* about this."

"She is," he agreed, tugging lightly on a strand of her reddish-blonde waves. "But she'll also be happy."

"Not as happy as I am," Bree beamed, nuzzled her nose against his. "As us."

He nuzzled her back, was about to kiss her again when a thought occurred to him.

"Wait." He frowned, pulled again. "You said Jackson asked you out, but you said no? How did he take it? I don't want him to think I'm rubbing it in his face or—"

"He knows about my feelings for you. I told him by way of explanation when I turned him down, and that I intended to tell you."

"You did?"

She nodded. "Sweetheart that he is, he understood, and agreed to keep it a secret until I'd said something to you. I think letting him know actually helped me finally tell you, because it held me accountable. It would've been unfair to him to tell him all of that, and then do nothing. It would've been cowardly of me."

Knowing his friend, Ryder could imagine exactly how it went down. And now the questioning glances Jax had let slip when looking at Bree recently made sense.

"I'll talk to him before we tell everyone," he said. "He deserves an explanation from me, too."

Bree's lips quirked in a pert little smile. "And what exactly are we telling everyone?"

He resisted the urge to nibble the smile off her face. "That we're together. We are together, aren't we?"

She tilted her head in mock consideration, then shrugged. "I'm down if you are."

God, she was adorable.

His smile turned heated, and he loved that she returned the look in equal measure.

This time when they came together, it was less rushed, but just as frenzied and explosive. He felt like a volcano about to erupt, and she felt like lava under his hands, which had made their way under her shirt and met smooth, soft skin.

She purred, and he didn't realize they were moving until her back hit the kitchen counter. As much as he wanted to move this to her bedroom, he also didn't want to move too fast.

He put his hands on her waist, reluctantly pulled back again.

"Bree—"

"Don't you dare go all gentlemanly on me now," Bree asserted, glaring up at him and gripping his shirt. "I can feel how much you want me, and I want you just as badly. I've waited too damn long for this. Don't make me wait another second."

She didn't have to ask him twice.

He hauled her up onto the countertop, drew her legs around his waist as she brought his mouth back to hers.

It was a marvel, he thought, that he was finally allowed to touch her. That her own slim, artistic hands were running all over him, making him quake with a desire he'd never known—never had for anyone but her.

There was no holding back now, she thought. His need awakened her own, and she was desperate to feel him, the years of pent up love and longing mixing into a sort of lustful high only he could fulfill.

Neither knew how long they stayed there, exploring each other, tugging off half their clothes, kissing and touching anywhere they could reach.

Eventually, he picked her up, carried her to the bed so they could discover each other anew.

And later, tangled together against her plush pillows, he turned to her, shifted them so he could see her face.

"I love you, Bree." It was sweet release to say it, out in the open and unencumbered by doubt.

Flushed with love and from lovemaking, Bree's smile was brilliant. "I love you, Ry. So much."

When he said nothing else, a pensive look taking over his face, she poked his bare stomach with her finger.

"What are you thinking?"

"I was thinking I'm not ready to share you with anyone."

She leaned up on her elbow, rested her head on her hand as she looked down at him, his dark hair sexily tousled. "What do you mean?"

His eyes trailed over her face. "What if we didn't tell anyone just yet, that we're together? Give ourselves some time, just the two of us, before we let all our friends and family into this."

"So you want to date in secret?"

"Not secret," he corrected. "Just low key. We've both waited so long for this, I just want some time with you to myself before we're inundated with questions."

She smiled softly. "I do like the sound of that. Though I doubt we'd be able to hide it from Ro."

He chuckled. "I think we're going to have to tell her, but she won't say anything if we ask her not to."

"That's a relief. How long would we wait to tell everyone else?"

"Not too long. I'm thinking a week," Ryder suggested. "And at the end of it, I'll meet up with Jackson so he's not blindsided."

Bree's brow furrowed a little. "I hope this doesn't come between you."

"It won't. But Levi might be a little upset with me if Jackson is hurt."

She pursed her lips, then slowly curved them in a wicked smile as she thought of something. "And what if he's distracted by a certain cousin of yours?"

He grinned. "We could make sure they're thrown together even more than they already are."

At her questioning look, he continued, "The Cubs are at home next weekend—what if we got a group together and went to the game?"

Bree hummed and wriggled closer to him, running her hands over his chest. "Sneaky."

"Indeed." His hands skimmed down her back to cup her bottom.

"Alright, then. One week," she declared. "Then no more hiding."

"No more hiding," he agreed, then flipped them so she lay under him, and she reached for him automatically.

This, he thought as his lips met hers in a languid, intoxicating kiss, was going to be one of the best weeks of his life.

AUTHOR'S NOTES

This story is my love letter to baseball.

I grew up playing softball, and sometimes practicing baseball with my brother, and I loved it; unfortunately, I didn't have much opportunity to play after high school, and I still miss it. So, a baseball story has been on my mind for quite some time.

I wrote most of the scene in which Farrow shows up at the Longhorns practice and ends up catching for them many years ago; I honestly don't remember how many, but probably around a decade. It wasn't Pride and Prejudice related at the time, it was just a scene in my head I had to get down on paper, an idea for something I might actually write someday.

Fast-forward to last year, when I was inspired to write a baseball P&P story. I vaguely knew what I wanted to write, but was struggling—until I found an old file I had saved, titled "Down the Heart."

I opened the file, and was immediately sucked in. I couldn't believe I'd written that, and was grateful I'd held onto it all these years, because it was the inspiration I needed, and I was able to rework it into the story I had in mind. (Hang on to your writing, kids. You might use it someday.)

Leagues like the one in this story do exist. The Chicagoland Adult Baseball Association is something I made up, but I based some of it on a combination of real-life adult leagues, namely the National Adult Baseball Association (NABA) Chicago Metro League, which influenced how I set up the league tiers (theirs are A, AA, and AAA), and the Midwest Suburban League, which helped me figure out the logistics of where games were played (Oakton Community College, among others, actually does host some Midwest Suburban League games).

Both leagues are labeled men's leagues. I couldn't find any information about whether or not either league would allow a woman to play, but since there was no overt rule against it (that I could see), I decided it could most certainly happen in my fictional story.

For those unfamiliar with the Chicago area, Morton Grove, where the Bennets live, is a suburb not too far outside the city; it's also close to Des Plaines, where Oakton Community College is. Morton Grove is also where the Netherfield Inn is, although the inn is not based on anything in real life.

The Nisei is, of course, a real place—and everything I wrote about it is true, right down to the chipped floor tiles and year-round Christmas decorations. And if you don't know what Malört is, you should count yourself lucky; although, if you do ever get a chance to try it, I recommend it just for the experience. (As long as you don't expect it to taste good. In fact, expect it to taste even worse than you think it will.)

The rally cheer Farrow and Bree instigate during the championship game, and the "Olé" cheer, are real cheers I remember from my own softball days. There are a few more I remember, but those were two that felt more natural to add in.

And just in case you missed all the baseball movie Easter Eggs, I quoted or made allusion to The Sandlot, The Bad News Bears, Major League, A League of Their Own, and Field of Dreams.

Thank you for joining me on this adventure, dear reader. It's been a hell of a ride.

—Mac

MORE BY MCKINLEY JAMES

A Turn of Events

Netherfield Vacation

Vitriol and Vineyards

Seaglass and Simplicity

My Reluctant Roommate

A Tale of Mistletoe Shenanigans

Snowed In

In the Stacks

Collections:

Incandescently

P&P Mashup Series:

A Pride & Prejudice Story

ABOUT THE AUTHOR

Of all Austen's characters, McKinley James identifies most with the quiet, socially awkward, and introverted Darcy. Pride and Prejudice is an old friend, and upon discovering the vast and fascinating world of Jane Austen Fan Fiction (and subsequently journeying down a year-long JAFF reading rabbit-hole) she decided to toss her own P&P stories into the fray. McKinley has a bachelor's degree in Creative Writing and, in her other life, works at a library. She lives in Chicago.

www.mckinleyjameswrites.com